Books by **Mapule Mokhawa:**

Jacaranda Blush
(*A journey back to purpose*)

The Book Queens
(*Queen Anea*)

Beauty for Ashes

A JOURNEY BACK TO PURPOSE

A novel

Mapule Mokhawa

ISBN: 978-0-7961-1809-7 (Print)
ISBN: 978-0-7961-1810-3 (eBook)

Contact author on: info.rhodaholdings@gmail.com
Instagram: @Mapule_Mo

Cover photo by Andre Moura via Canva

Scripture quotations used in the book are taken from Holy Bible; *New Living Translation*, Copyright© 1996, 2004. Used by permission of Tyndale House Publishers, Inc., Carol Stream Illinois 60188. All rights reserved.
Scripture quotations are from the ESV® Bible (The Holy Bible, English Standard Version®), copyright © 2001 by Crossway Bibles, a publishing ministry of Good News Publishers. Used by permission. All rights reserved.
Scripture quotations marked (KJV) taken from the King James Version (KJV). Public domain.

My frame was not hidden from You, when I was being made in secret...

ACKNOWLEDGEMENTS

The support, purchase, feedback and reviews I received after the release of Jacaranda Blush have opened a way for this book and I am grateful to every person for that.

To my young aunt, you have no idea how much I appreciate what you did in those first few weeks. It's sitting deep in my heart.
I'm grateful to my parents Mmatilo and Bethuel Sekgoka, and all my family, friends and everyone in my circle. Your support is humbling.
To my mother-in-law, thank you for making me your own.

To my husband, you are a gift in my life. I appreciate your patience and how you make room for my dreams.
I'd be in trouble if I didn't mention my children by name, Kuvhanganani, Unarine and Rinaye. They've also had to hold back their chatter while I worked on the book.
And lastly, a special thank you to every person who is taking a moment to read this book.

CHAPTER 1

Mmakoma placed her glass on the kitchen counter and rubbed its stem like she was counting the seconds before he would make it to the door. She had seen him park from the balcony where she was standing before she strode to the kitchen to unlock the door and wait.

"Afternoon," he said, walking in after a brief knock. He was in a short-sleeved brown shirt and brown golfing shorts. It was typical of him to have his bottoms match whatever he had on top.

He smiled and she smiled back before drawing her wine glass to herself. He still had that inviting effect to him, and it had gotten stronger of late. Something about him was grooming out well, a new aura, a tap to his walk, flavour to his laughter, a sparkle to his smile. At a different time, she would have made a fitting move but that sparkling thing on his hand unsettled her. It was a loud declaration of him never wanting to be with her again.

"Papa." Dipuo ran up to jump on him. He lifted her up and spun her in the air. Mogau followed behind and gently hugged him. She was beginning to think of herself as a big girl.

"Are you good?" he asked Mmakoma. His daughters pulled him from either side. They jabbered for his attention with all sorts of stories and he engaged them.

"Yeah, sure," she said with that 'don't mind me' look on her face. She sipped again and continued to watch what could have been a perfect family playing out in front of her. Lekau wore fatherhood well. They could have had a beautiful family, but he threw it all out of the window by marrying that girl.

"Gather your things girls. We are leaving now." The girls raced to their bedroom leaving their parents to themselves. Lekau tried to find a place for his hands while Mmakoma sipped red wine, slowly savouring it in.

"So…" she broke the ice. "How's married life?"

As he rubbed his mobile phone to keep at something, the question was a welcome distraction. His mouth was beginning to open up when the roughing sound of Dipuo's pink suitcase grabbed both their attention. Mogau was right behind with hers. It had become inherent that whenever Lekau asked for their suitcases to be packed, they would be going straight to Lekau's house in Pretoria, not the Makwela homestead where they had separate bedrooms with tonnes of clothes. If Rebecca Makwela wasn't decorating spaces or on top of a horse, she was shopping for her grandchildren.

"Papa please open the car," Dipuo paused.

"It's open baby," he said before moving his eyes back to Mmakoma.

"It's good," he tilted his face to search her eyes.

"Good for you," she sipped some more and fixed her one shouldered black dress. It had short black frills going under her shoulder and all the way around. She felt good in it. It marked her beautiful silhouette perfectly and its expense was adequately justified.

"Thanks." He paused and looked her in the eye. A sign of genuine gratitude. But that gaze seared into her heart. She remembered it. It had melted it before. Now, strangely, it pierced pain deep inside.

"Nat has died," she filled the empty silence that was thickening with every second.

"Oh," he frowned. Mmakoma dropped her face and shed a tear about it for the first time. She shook her head to compose herself. It must have been the wine she was having so early in the day.

"I'm so sorry," he came around the kitchen

counter and took away the wine glass from her hand. He held her to himself and patted her gently. This always comforted her. It comforted her again now.

"Visit your mom. Don't be by yourself here." He stepped back as she began to calm down. She giggled dryly. Alice Komane could give comfort to everyone else but her own daughter. She believed that she would be better equipped if she mastered how to pull it together and to keep the display of weakness at bay. That was how she trained her. It was a commendable skill for a doctor to possess.

"I'll be fine. Cindy is on her way. We are going to his funeral today," she said. Khabonina was also coming back in the evening. They didn't talk much but Mmakoma was beginning to suspect that she had gotten herself a boyfriend somewhere in the neighbourhood.

"Good," he breathed out relief. "Let me leave you then."

She watched him pick his key and walk out. A pout of thin saliva filled her mouth and with the same speed, she swallowed it. Something unexplainable was emerging out of him. He oozed with it. It was nothing tangible but somehow, it made him breath-takingly noticeable. Lekau has always been somewhat appealing, but he was getting seasoned with age and maturity. There's just something about a man who can commit.

But why couldn't he ever afford her the same

kind of commitment after being with him for close to a decade? A simple girl came along, and he proposed at a whim. She was not prettier, nor smarter, no degree behind her name, no car, no sense of style, absolutely nothing on her.

"I still think that you must fight for that man," Cindy said when Mmakoma told her that Lekau was there earlier to fetch the girls.

"He belongs to someone else now," Mmakoma muttered as she grabbed a black cape and black fascinator. She stepped out of her pink slippers into her black, red bottoms before covering her lips with some lip gloss. Then she touched up her perfume, smelling good was synonymous to her name.

"I'm tired of seeing death," Mmakoma said to Cindy looking at the expansive number of graves around them. The cemetery felt like a dusty weird place and to think that Nathaniel's body was going to join the rest of the lifeless people all around them was unimaginable. It still didn't feel like it was true. He was still so young and full of life.

Paul, his cousin, tried to explain what happened to him but her shock couldn't let her process anything. It was a car accident, that much she had grasped. Her mind alluded it to drunken driving as she slowly began to think about it. Paul was already off the line, so she never got to be sure-sure. It was not unlike Nat to be in a drunken driving mess and he never learnt.

The sun rays blazed the skin and the heat was hard to bear. Cindy had a small umbrella and she tried to pull her in, but it didn't seem to help. Her umbrella was way too small to cover both of them. Mmakoma tried to move so she could turn her face away from the sun, but her Loubotins were pressed into the soft ground. It irritated her. Such things ruined the finish of good shoes. The makers of red bottoms must have not had the soft grounds of cemeteries in mind when they designed them.

A sudden and sharp lament pulled everyone's attention. It was hysterical. And surreal. The lady only had one friend to hold and comfort her.

There was another one who started crying into Mmakoma and Cindy's ears as the men threw dust over Nat's casket.

"Your friends must keep it together," Cindy whispered.

"My friends?" Mmakoma pulled her face.

"You know there's many of you," Cindy smiled cunningly. Mmakoma pouted her lips and shook her head. Nat was a man who could never be trusted around any woman. He was incredibly funny, and equally as charming and charismatic. It used to hurt her when she still had hopes of him changing, but as the years passed and she grew wiser, she started playing his game too. No hearts got involved, just pleasant exchange of bodily fluids.

Nat's mother sat next to his sisters under one of the gazebos. Her face was red from crying. Perhaps from the heat too. Except for a wrinkle or two, and a few greys below her hat, she hadn't changed much.

Mmakoma noticed one thing though, the woman was an aged version of Dipuo walking around. It was odd, and eccentric. It was "not make sure" (not making sense/ delusional. Not how it's supposed to be). Even the way she moved her face to make different facial expressions.

She covered her lips. It was a secret only she, Lekau and Nathaniel knew. Nat never wanted children. He was never responsible enough to begin with.

Her stomach twirled at the memory of the day she went to the Makwela's with Dipuo still inside her. Caiphas and Rebecca were delighted that they were going to be grandparents again. Their joy was contagious. It made her happy too. But Lekau sat there quietly. She recalled how he placed his face between his hands as his elders danced to an addition to their clan. Rebecca even dragged him and forced him into celebration. He did, even in his reluctance.

It amazed her how he rose to the party and fathered Dipuo nothing less than he has Mogau. Moreover, he kept her secret with honour, not exposing it even to his own family.

She whispered to Cindy that they were to go back to her place immediately after the funeral and not join all mourners at the family home. She told her that she would rather avoid the counterfeit gestures of sympathy and pretence comradery that came with funerals. But it was the sight of Nathaniel's mother after so many years that compelled her. The way in which looking at her felt like looking at her daughter.

In all her sinning, which she was going to pray about in church the next day anyway, there was one that she was incapable of committing. That is, to look Nat's mother in the eye and to see her pain of losing a son yet withhold that she had a grandchild by him. She wasn't there yet.

"Nat was a proper ladies' man. Three girlfriends crying in one funeral," Cindy joked again as they drove on Kerk Street on their way to Flora Park where Mmakoma lived. Her focus was on the nursery they were passing. The thought of flowers took her back to the reality of Nathaniel being gone.

"Oh, please Cindy." She shook her head that made her lack of interest clear.

"Nat was a ladies' man, you know it friend," Cindy said.

"Isn't it too soon to be saying such about someone who has left this world?" Mmakoma mumbled.

"What else do you remember him for?" Cindy giggled.

"A whole lot more. At some point I thought the two of us were going to spend a lifetime together. You didn't know him the way that I did," Mmakoma's eyes were teary. Cindy looked at her friend and decided to keep driving silently. On a different day, she would have said more, and they would have laughed about it.

"MJ do you have enough champagne or wine?" Cindy asked as they passed Spar.

"I never run out of red wine, you know that," she smiled.

Safari River Estate was designed to have grey and white buildings that were grouped in fours. Two homes on top, two at the bottom. There were numerous of these blocks of buildings in the estate, suitable for lovers of both luxury and communal living.

Mmakoma pulled off her stilettos as soon as they made it into her apartment. The white tiles had a cooling effect on her feet after hours in stilettos. Cindy gently tossed hers next to the coffee table and walked to get some wine glasses. She warmed up some left-over pizza.

"You need to get a man," she said to Mmakoma as she placed both wine glasses on the coffee table. "Can't be in a desert for that long. It's not healthy."

"I'm the health expert here and I can confirm that I'm absolutely fine," Mmakoma jested, touching her brown wig that was slicked all the way to where her bra strap circled her upper body.

"Doctors still need other doctors" Cindy filled both their glasses and handed Mmakoma one. Mmakoma sipped over Cindy's words. It wasn't physical intimacy that she longed for.

"Now that Nat's gone and Lekau has made some horrible decisions that exclude you, it might be time to move on, don't you think?" Cindy said.

"My heart has moved on Cindy. I just don't have a man to prove it."

For Mmakoma, relationships always ended as extra work, even the ones that were not supposed to be serious. There was always something to fix. They were always great on the first few dates, then when you get to know them, it's game on.

She wanted to mention something about Tafadzwa but decided not to. People always said foreign men were ten times better, much to her disappointment. She pulled breath and rolled her eyes thinking about it.

"Be nice to Muzi. He's a catch," Cindy said before chewing some pizza. Mmakoma gave her friend a look. She knew very well how Muzi was. He was constantly making his interest obvious and his inclined choice in scent and good apparel made her consider forgiving how full of himself the guy was.

Self-absorption and namedropping were all he could contribute to a conversation.

"He's a catch to you, not me." She shut Cindy off.

There had been a time when she hoped to fix things with Lekau, especially after the mess she created by bringing Nat into his house, but Lekau never got over that. He went on to marry that plain girl instead, making nothing of the number of times that she had also forgiven him.

At first, she thought it was a rebound relationship, especially with her not being the type Lekau always went for. He had a taste for cosmopolitan women, girls who knew where to shop and what to shop for. His wife fell short of that cut.

The first time Mmakoma met Mmathapelo, she wore flat pumps that could have been bought at Marabastad. That left her with renewed confidence that she would get the father of her children back.

Lekau had had his flings like all men do but he was stable and reliable, a good father for the girls. The gift of a loving home with a mother and father in the house was something she had always wanted the girls to have, but Lekau saw it fit to take it away. It was pathetic to even recall how he told her to go and be with Nat. That was childish of him, spiteful to say the least.

No woman wanted a man like Nat to father her children. Perhaps it was her own anger talking but Nathaniel made it clear that he never saw himself as a father and when she fell pregnant with their first child, he persuaded her to terminate, and she agreed. It broke her, but it also broke their relationship.

"I'm not going to go looking for a man Cindy." She snapped out of her thoughts and answered her friend. She gobbled half her glass of wine in. She took a breathing break before gobbling the last half. Cindy side-eyed her.

"What? I'm thirsty," she laughed.

"Hm, drown all your sorrows girl," Cindy pulled a dry smile. Mmakoma laughed before touching her phone for the first time in a few hours. She noticed a missed call from her father. She kept scrolling. The man would smell her intoxication from as far as Polokwane was to the Cape wine farms. It was better to call him back the next day with the helm of sobriety to her responses. David Komane could never tolerate a woman drinking. To this day, he had no knowledge that his wife, Alice often enjoyed wine.

There was also a text from Boikarabelo; **Hi, how was the funeral? How are you?**

CHAPTER 2

The buzzing sound of excited teenagers filled the stadium as Thabo scored a goal for their school. It was a goal that solidified their lead and gave them a score of three to one. It was going to take above average tact for the other team to catch up within the twenty minutes that remained.

"I see how well you've done for Dinaledi Secondary School." A familiar female voice spoke in his ear. He shut his eyes hoping he didn't hear well.

"Sharon." He turned to find her face.

"What?" she laughed at his reaction.

"You never went to kids' soccer games." He pulled a reluctant smile.

"If I knew that I was going to find you here, I'd

have started long ago."

"Mmh." He moved his body. She didn't say anything but her presence behind him brought him memories of their time together. He would have cherished the reminder, but shame amassed him.

"Your boys are in form. Well done," she said.

"They have a fantastic coach." He didn't look at her but hoped she would leave. She stayed. Until the final whistle.

The stadium filled up with jubilant songs of victory steered by youthful teenage voices. Kamano got up and clapped hands for them. His face was soaked in pride.

Two teachers from the other school came to shake his hand and congratulate him. Then a parent came forth as well. The stands began to empty but Sharon was still there, waiting for only what she knew.

Kamano turned to say goodbye.

"How about lunch?" Sharon said.

"I'm afraid I cannot. I have to..."

"For old times," she interjected. "I still need closure."

Kamano looked at his feet and began tapping his takkies. He had two hearts about it, "I suppose you do."

A smile covered her beautiful round face.

"I have a place in mind. You will love it."

"Mmh," he groaned.

The place was a café not too far from where the soccer tournament was hosted. He parked his car besides hers and checked if his bank card was still inside his black tracksuit pocket. There were some bank notes too. Sharon never paid for anything when they were together. She wasn't going to start now.

"How has it been without her?" she started.

His eyes hit hers for the first time since their encounter at the stadium. There wasn't a match to occupy himself with this time. There was no crowd to forge noises that washed off the absurdity of being together again.

Sharon was eventually going to locate him. It was in her nature. She was going to seek answers. She was going to seek retribution if not retrieval of what they once shared.

He had since changed numbers and moved schools. Her failure to locate him all these years was most probably intentional. He couldn't have been that hard to trace. He still moved within teaching circles. It was no longer in the village in Ga-Semenya, but still, he was within Polokwane. It couldn't have been too hard.

"You miss her, don't you?" she sounded genuine. But talking about Lesego was off the table, especially with her.

"How are you?" His evasion was as clear as day.

"I'm okay," she smiled realising what he had just done. "Life hasn't been the same without you."

"Mmh." He curled his lips and moved his chin up.

"I miss you."

"Mmh."

"Say something Kamano," she said.

"I'm here to listen to you," he said. She placed her phone on the table and placed her hand below her cheeks. She wore a colourful woollen summer dress with red sandals. She was a thick curvy woman of bright complexion.

"I've tried seeing other people afterwards but none of them was like you. We were beautiful together," she paused, and waited for him to say something again.

"I suppose that's a compliment," he jested uncomfortably. There were a lot of things that happened between the last time he was with her and now. She was still as dazzling. And he was now a single man. But something in him couldn't find settlement.

"Are you seeing someone now?"

He hesitated around the question.

"You said you needed closure."

"I do."

"How can I help you find it?"

She placed her cup in the saucer and gazed at it for a while.

"Do you miss me?"

"I do," he said. He missed her. He missed companionship. He missed being with a woman.

"Why don't we try again?"

"I cannot," he said apologetically.

"Why not? Is there someone else?"

"There's no one."

It was easier to say that there was someone else. Maybe it would ward her away this time. But he had overcome lying.

"I need to go."

He pushed himself off the seat, trying hard to be as gentle as he could. He took the bank notes out of his pocket and placed them on the table.

"I really need to go," he repeated to her maudlin eyes and his heart ached for her.

CHAPTER 3

Mmakoma buried herself between her arms that were squared over her desk that morning and let out.

"God, this job feels meaningless, my life feels meaningless," she wailed pulling out pink tissue to wipe her tears away. She girded herself up for the day. Her supply of tears was now out as she moved her eyes from certificate to certificate on the wall.

Someone peeped into her office. It was Dr Boikarabelo Kgopa.

"Ready for the day?" Boikarabelo asked, still at the door with coffee in her hand.

"What choice do I have?"

She swung her light brown leathered chair and pulled her white coat from her rack and wore it over her tailored blouse. Boikarabelo began leading the way out of Mmakoma's practice rooms. They passed Charlene who was on the phone behind the reception counter. It sounded like she was following up on an unpaid account. Mmakoma waved and passed with Boikarabelo.

"I know a place not too far from the shopping complex where you can get your nails done at a good price. They do an excellent job for what they charge," Mmakoma suggested at the sight of Boikarabelo's undone nails.

"My hands are working hands," she replied.

"Nails don't need to be long, just done," Mmakoma said as Boikarabelo threw her cup into a bin. Undone nails took away from good first impressions, but Boikarabelo seemed unbothered by the fact. Hers were nails of a nail biter.

If she was going to try going with Mmakoma anywhere, she needed to work on her appearance. She wasn't quite the type of person Mmakoma would befriend, but then Mmakoma hardly ever added to her list of friends.

Her friend Cindy was the complete opposite. She had friends from everywhere. When she mentioned Boikarabelo's attempts to befriend her, Cindy said it might be admiration that made her try so hard.

"I don't know," Boi mumbled.

"That excuse about your hands being working hands is just not it," Mmakoma said. Mrs Mokoena interrupted them with a greeting. She was paddling a patient on a wheelchair into the elevator.

They smiled at her and continued to walk in comfortable silence.

"How was the funeral?" Boi asked.

Mmakoma's neck tickled as she recalled the blue-ticked message she never bothered to reply to for four days.

"Well, I looked great at the funeral. That's the only nice thing about the past few days of my life," she giggled.

"Death is something we just never get used to," Boikarabelo spoke softly as they arrived at the ward.

"I see people at their worst every day and I have to bring my best in every one of those days. I have to listen to them, help them and even heal them. It gets too much," Mmakoma whispered back in a way that nobody else could hear. They had mastered the art of conversing at low voices in certain parts of the hospital.

"Sometimes they die. As if I haven't seen enough of death in my life. It's like death surrounds me, it follows me. Whenever I care about something, that thing dies." Mmakoma breathed heavily to suppress tears.

"We don't have an easy job," Boikarabelo said.

None of the younger doctors that Mmakoma had mentored before matched her proficiency and sanguinity. The lines of a master and her apprentice were always clear with them but never with

Boikarabelo. She was too sure of herself to be bothered by the limits of any hierarchy.

"There's purpose to what we do. People search for that their entire lives," Boi said casually, yet softly in a very low reassuring tone. Mmakoma stopped at her. She wanted to tell her how it all felt like a lie to her. The wards drained the very last of vigour she had. Only her work ethic still drove her legs to bring her body to work every day.

"We are about to save lives, that's a big deal." Boikarabelo was enthusiastic. She wasn't just there to gain experience in cardiology and paediatrics. She was convinced of her presence filling a specific void. In her world, she was a piece of a puzzle.

Mmakoma picked up a file. It was of a child whose body was burnt from jumping into a hot tub of water. Her wounds had been attended to, but the child had an ailing heart from birth. There were concerns about the effect of the trauma. Mmakoma carefully scanned her file, and then smiled at the six-year-old. She smiled back with the warmest smile Mmakoma had seen all day. She had a look at her wounds, then checked the pain meds she had already been given. She pulled the nurse on duty for further explanation before assessing issues of her heart.

There was also a man who had experienced heart failure while driving on the highway. He sustained some injury. Car accident patients were common during the festive time of the year.

Mmakoma saw a few other patients before taking a break and driving out from Hospital Street, down Landros Mare Street and eventually into Limpopo Mall. It was a refreshing escape with healthy looking people all over. No wounds to handle, no smell of medication, just people who were dressed well to shop.

She got herself a sandwich and juice. Then a bashful feeling took over her mind. Boikarabelo always bought her food and snacks. Not once had she gotten her anything. She picked up another sandwich and bottle of juice and went to the till.

She noticed that a new craft shop had been opened next to the exit. There were all sorts of pieces made by people with their own hands. One mural was made from cool drink can-openers. She stopped to admire the kind of craftiness that meticulously went into it. She thought of all the places she could hang something like that. It had been long since she stopped to appreciate works of art. It had also been long since she stopped to put effort into a hobby, or anything else besides medicine. The vocation and her relationship with it had consumed much of her life.

She phoned her father while walking to the parking lot. He was now in Johannesburg where Komane Civils had a construction site. She promised to visit the construction site before saying goodbye and hanging up.

Driving back to work, a red VW Polo came from her right and ignored the flashing red light. It was her turn, but the driver of the Polo went ahead and took the road space for himself. Mmakoma hit the brakes to let him pass. She also hit her hooter in a sprout of heated irritation. She stuck out her finger and shouted profanely. The man smiled from his open window.

"Ncaa, you don't even have an aircon," she said, more to herself than him. He couldn't have heard her, but still, nobody opened their windows so much unless they had a weak aircon.

It raged Mmakoma even more when he stopped on the side to look at his phone. He must have been lost.

What was the point if you were going to stop? Idiot!

She drove past him to stop at the next traffic lights that were red against her.

She shot a look at her rear-view mirror. The red VW Polo was now behind her. The fool again. Could he be following me? She had seen psychopaths behave that way in movies.

The man drove behind her, maintaining a short distance. She slowed down for him to pass but he didn't. At the small traffic circle outside hospital, she indicated to the right and the Polo indicated right too. At this point, her mind was going in a thousand directions.

Immense relief flushed through her when she went into reserved parking and the man drove on.

She pulled out her phone and typed to Boikarabelo - **I've got a sandwich for you. Are you in your office?**

The text followed a several of Boikarabelo's texts that Mmakoma never replied to.

Yes. Thank you so much. – Boikarabelo replied promptly. Mmakoma pulled down the mirror on her car and watched herself brush her silky-smooth weave before tying it in a loose ponytail. She assessed her chocolate brown skin to see if all the pimples from her period were gone.

She noticed a towering figure coming closer and closer. The man stopped near her window and bended down. She cussed inside her lungs. Then she noticed who it was. She rolled her window down a few centimetres.

"What?" she said. She was not going to give away the slightest sign of fear. The hospital cameras and security would catch his behind if he dared to try anything sinister.

"A woman as gorgeous as you shouldn't go around sticking her finger out like that," he said. His voice was calm, a melodious baritone.

"F you." Mmakoma lashed out more profanity towards him. She added a stern and fearless face to it.

"Hm," he laughed. It vexed her. It got her boiling. She rolled her window up and the idiot smiled on the other side before walking away. He was a man of a large stature, like that of a heightened rugby player.

She sanitized her hands and picked up the food and her black Chanel handbag. She had black formal trousers with a tailored black blouse on. On her feet were gold loafers and a gold Chanel brooch was on the left side of her chest area. Above it, she was going to clip her nametag back on.

She greeted some nurses and cleaners at reception and went up the stairs to the section where intern doctors sat.

Softly, she knocked before letting herself inside. The door was half open. Boikarabelo wasn't in the office but there was a man.

It was the idiot again. Mmakoma's nose and lips lifted, she made no effort to hide her disdain.

"Where is Dr Kgopa?" she asked him.

"Bathroom," the man wore a wry smile. It was annoying. "She'll be back in no time."

"Tell her that Dr Komane was here."

She tamed herself from saying something about his clothes. He would have deserved it. Who wore a red jersey over a navy-blue shirt that looked like it had been washed over a hundred times? The nerve to walk around like he owned the place while dressed like a postman who last went shopping decades ago was unbelievable. She turned around and went to her practice rooms.

There she had small talk with Charlene before going into her office. In there, she went through her mail and started to make a few notes on her notepad.

"I was told that you came looking for me," Boikarabelo interrupted her.

"Yeah, there was a man in your office," Mmakoma raised her face. It would be thirty-five minutes before patients with appointments would start flooding her practice.

"That was my brother, Kamano," Boikarabelo explained.

"Sorry to say this but your brother is an idiot. We had a little altercation on the road because he's a bad driver and he smiled about it. Can you believe it? I could have crushed his ant-sized car with my 4Matic you know," Mmakoma said. Boikarabelo laughed.

"He's not that bad. He said that you seemed like a hot-tempered woman," Boikarabelo.

"How dare he? He doesn't even know me."

"Looks like you two are starting off on the wrong foot."

Boikarabelo bit her sandwich and sipped juice.

"We are not starting off anything. The thought of seeing him again," Mmakoma cringed. "You must tell him to dress his age."

"Yeah, he doesn't dress too well," Boikarabelo

laughed.

CHAPTER 4

Fake greenery and silvery ornaments cheered the corridors of the hospital with a festal mood. Mmakoma smiled at the nurse who touched a wreath in appreciation. The door opened and Boikarabelo came in with a clipboard in her hand. Her gaze was fixed on Mmakoma all the way.

"Dr J, our suspicions about Mrs Rooi are confirmed." She began to update Mmakoma about a patient who was reacting negatively to treatment.

"Does she have any endothelial dysfunction? Thyroiditis maybe?"

Mmakoma latched on to the clipboard that was in Boikarabelo's hand and studied it. Mrs Rooi's immune system was beginning to deteriorate and

Boikarabelo leaned on Mmakoma's experience for a course of action.

"Her doctor has confirmed thyroiditis," Boikarabelo said.

"Previous treatments?" Mmakoma asked. "Do you have all details?"

"Yes," Boikarabelo pointed some details on the board.

"Great," Mmakoma made some notes and handed the clipboard back as her phone vibrated in her pocket. "We can take it from here," she looked for Boikarabelo's eyes before drawing away to take the phone call.

"Mommy please send me money. I want to go to the mall with my friends," Dipuo said on the line.

"Hi Dipuo, how are you?" Mmakoma responded to her youngling, insisting that she learnt to greet first, the same way Aunty Tsakani had taught her.

"Hi mommy. Did you hear what I asked?"

"Yes, I heard you. Why don't you ask your father there? When did you start having friends that go to malls anyway?"

"Daddy already gave me money. I want from you, please mommy. I want to mix the money and buy myself a big doll house."

"No Dipuo. Where's your sister?"

"She's in daddy's bedroom with Mmathapelo. You want to talk to her?"

"No, I'll talk to her another time," Mmakoma.

"Mmathapelo says we will be doing something nice for Christmas. She says it's a surprise." Dipuo sounded excited.

"Okay my dear. Keep well, and if anyone bothers you or hits you, let mommy know as soon as possible, okay?" Mmakoma said.

"Okay mommy. I love you mommy."

"I love you too my baby, bye."

"Your kids will still be away on Christmas?" Boikarabelo had been listening to her conversation. Mmakoma cleared her throat, but Boikarabelo's eyes were set on the clipboard, her hand moving back and forth with a pen.

Mmakoma rolled a lock of hair and turned her head to look at what Boikarabelo was jotting down. She wrestled the apprehension that was forming in her mind over having yet another Christmas alone. Her childhood had been filled with so many of those. She knew the sadness of it and the loneliness of it.

Only in her mind existed moments she and her twin brother could have shared. She had created those, none of them were ever real. But they filled her childhood and kept her yearning suppressed.

The eight or seven Christmases with the Makwela's had fooled her into thinking that her entire adult life would be like that. She had gained a family. Rebecca Makwela had pulled her under her own wing and made her one of her own. But it all disappeared with a breakup. Well, not the breakup. Not quite. It was Lekau's marriage to Mmathapelo that ended it all. His audacity to replace her like she was nothing still discomposed her, two babies later. Not two, not really but Dipuo and Mogau are a package deal.

"I've got training in Johannesburg this afternoon. I've got to go," she said to Boikarabelo.

"Cool," Boikarabelo replied softly.

Mmakoma refreshed herself at the bathrooms and changed into white trousers and a black vest. Her feet were braced in brown sandals and she moved her items into a double knot bag by Bottega Veneta. It was a brown bag, one that had leather threads from one knot to the other. It gave her that sophisticated gardener look.

She drove non-stop until the off-ramp going into M81, leading into Bryanston. She got herself a pack of biltong and some juice at the petrol station before driving to the office park for the conference.

She settled on one of the benches outside before someone came to sit next to her.

"I'm Anne," she said.

Mmakoma smiled at her and quickly read the name card on her. She loved it when doctors introduced themselves with their own names devoid of titles.

"I'm Mmakoma," she smiled back.

"I'm sorry, you say Ma...?" Anne begged pardon.

Mmakoma considered telling Anne to just call her Janet, but then she wasn't going to make it too easy for her. She preferred to be called Mmakoma and that was how she was going to have it.

"Mm-uh-ko-muh," she repeated slowly. Anne repeated after her. She got it. Even the tone was spot on. Their chatter went on until conference started. It ended at 5pm, to resume at 7am the next morning.

Her hotel wasn't too far from the venue. It had a restaurant with a deck that allowed an experience of the Johannesburg sun setting. It was a bright reddish-orange light that disappeared into the sky leaving a calming twilight behind.

The restaurant offered a sizeable range of wines alongside their scrumptious a la carte. This was a dream for an oenophile like her. The waiter told her about a wine she had desired to taste but could never find in Polokwane and she instantly ordered a bottle.

She held the stem of the glass and gently took in the aroma of the fermented red grapes before sipping and holding it in her mouth to swirl around. She pleasantly shook her head at the waiter. It was worth every penny.

"A connoisseur of wine." A light-skinned man in a navy suit greeted her.

"Hi." She turned and smiled at him, with lines forming between her eyes.

"You don't remember me? Do you?" he said.

Her brows rose, then she squinted her eyes, "I'm sorry, I don't."

"You wouldn't. You always sat in front at med school," he said.

"You were in my class?"

"Yes," he said.

"I'm sorry. This is embarrassing," she laughed and shook her head.

"Dr Rhulani Mabasa." He stretched out his hand.

"That rings a bell." She matched his handshake and giggled.

"Are you by yourself? Mind if I join you?"

"Not at all," Mmakoma said. Rhulani pulled out a seat by her side and her olfactory system went into immediate surveillance. It was Amouage Opus that he had on. She could never mistake that scent.

"Mmakoma Komane." She introduced herself even though there was no need.

"I saw you at the conference earlier." He sat down.

"You're also here for it?" she asked.

"Yeah. We've got to keep learning you know," he said.

"It was great seeing a familiar face. You haven't changed one bit."

"I can't say the same about you," she laughed.

"A couple of gym trips, three kids and a divorce later. I think you have a point," he jested.

"You changed for the better."

"And you?" he cleared his throat. "Any children or spouse?"

"I'm single with two daughters;" she replied. The breeze pushed a couple of locks of hair to her face and she gently removed them with her hand. The waiter also came to check on them. He refilled her wine and took Rhulani's order. "I always thought you'd be married to a big politician by now," Rhulani said playfully. Mmakoma cracked up in laughter.

"I mean you drove a G-Wagon to school. You were untouchable."

"I had no idea that I was untouchable," she said.

"What made it worse was that you always got the highest marks. None of us would dare try our luck with you," Rhulani.

How she wished that at least one of them could have tried. Maybe it would have saved her from all the mess she ended up getting herself into.

But then her younger self wouldn't have understood what intimidation was to a man. As perfect as she may have seemed at that time, her life was permanently winding into a web of complications. Nathaniel took over in her mind and heart and all her innocence was lost.

CHAPTER 5

"I'm ready to go." Those were Khabonina's words the day before, on the twenty-fourth. Her two bags stacked by her side guaranteed her departure. One was full and small. The other big and almost empty. She was going to shop when she got off at Park Station before being in transit again, from Johannesburg to Kwa-Zulu Natal.

Now being left alone with the reminder of Christmas all around stirred her loneliness. It was grappling. She thought of calling Rhulani one more time, just to chat, but he hadn't returned any of her calls.

She didn't want to feel any sort of way about it. She was a grown woman now. Feeling used was for young girls. There was nothing he could have taken away from her. Besides, she might never ever see him again.

She poured herself a glass. She was going to numb that yearning down and lull herself to sleep. She could drink as much as she desired because there was no face to see that day.

She fought her tears and they succumbed. The heat of the wine and its tickle in her system did not erase that enigmatic longing. She had everything that money could buy, but her desire for closeness had no price tag, she was beginning to realise that. Not even her beautiful body could buy that. If it could, Rhulani would be with her now, Lekau would be with her, Tafadzwa would be with her. She had parents but she never quite had them.

Standing on her balcony, she swiped her phone and dialled her father's number. It was better to do it before she was too far into her bottle.

"Merry Christmas dad," she said.

"Merry Christmas my girl," his voice was thick and reassuring. Loving as always.

"Where are you? I miss you," she said.

"I'm in Bloubergstrand. I'm planning to walk on the beach in an hour. If the weather is right, I might try jet skiing," he said.

"Oh," she rubbed her denim skirt wondering when her old man left Johannesburg.

She always wore blue denim and something white

on top on Christmas. It brought her close to her fondest memory. A time when Alice was out of the country and Aunty Tsakani, her childhood nanny went to the village with her. It was the first time she experienced the festivity of Christmas village-style. She danced to fast paced Shangaan songs and wiggled the xibelani that belonged to Nkateko, Aunty's daughter. Even though there had been no need, Aunty had bought her new clothes that matched Nkateko's clothes. A white T-shirt and denim shorts with diamante around the pockets. Both their sandals were pink, and they were like twins that day. But Alice later expressed a disapproval of it and tossed those clothes in the bin. No daughter of hers was going to be seen in cheap lines.

It was only later in life that she had the closest sense to Aunty Tsakani's motherly warmth. It was with Lekau's mother, Rebecca Makwela. Even when Lekau wanted nothing to do with her, Rebecca still treated her with love and acceptance.

She hung up from the call with her father and stared at the motionless parking lot. The estate was quiet, and empty. Perhaps meaningless conversations with sick people would have made a better Christmas day.

She shook her wine glass in admiration of her dearest friend, her wine. It hit all the palettes in her mouth, just the way that she loved it. The ability of good red wine to fully satisfy all senses of taste was unmatched. She loved it.

A white car passed and being the only moving thing in the estate at that time, it caught her eye. Some breeze brushed over her and the scent of her own perfume delicately waved through the air. It was one of the perfumes her mother brought from London in June. Something about that top smell of vanilla backed by oud and citrus uplifted her mood. Gourmand scents were her thing, followed by floral and powdery scents.

She wondered if her mother would come bearing luxe perfumes when she returned from Germany this time.

She tapped her foot that was clad in pink Hermes sandals. She had bought the shoes as part of a build-up to gain the privilege to buy her first Birkin bag some years ago.

A call from Boikarabelo came in again. She had invited her to her family's Christmas party, and she did not decline. Neither did she accept. But she had already talked herself out of the idea. It was giving desperation. Boikarabelo was not her equal and she preferred that line thick and clear.

"Doctor J, I'm coming to fetch you," she said.

"Naa, I'm already cooking. I'll be perfectly fine. Thanks."

"I know you're alone. I'm coming to fetch you," Boikarabelo said. Mmakoma quickly built up a story in her mind. Something to redeem her from the shame of not having anyone to spend Christmas with. But she had promised herself to fight any desire to unnecessarily lie. She said nothing.

Boikarabelo arrived in her brother's red Polo. The girl was pushy. Mmakoma switched off her stove, spilled her glass of wine into the sink and picked up her handbag and jumped into the red Polo. They went to Seshego.

Mavis Kgopa was a woman in her sixties. She welcomed her with a warm hug and her brown curly wig scratched her face a little.

Her home was well set for Christmas. She had a jumping castle for the kids in her back yard, and a colourful Christmas theme under a white stretch tent for kids. They had slides, face paintings and a host of games to entertain them.

In the front was a more relaxed set up with white ottomans and sofas made from wooden pallets over a green fake grass carpet. The food was placed inside round silver warmers, the kind you would find at a wedding.

Mrs Mavis Kgopa's singing marked the start of their family Christmas. The woman's voice was like that of the women who sang for Ncandweni Christ Ambassadors. It was matured, the kind of voice you imagine singing, "It's a wonderful day, oh yes, it's a wonderful day…"

Her singing was brief and soulful. Mmakoma

wasn't familiar with the song she sang but she wondered what it would be like to hear its decorated version.

"Afternoon family and all our friends and guests," Mrs Kgopa began to talk.

"I just want to welcome all of you to my home. What a pleasure to see each other again," she said.

"We have chosen to use this day to remember His birth," Mavis pointed her finger upwards. "We are a mere product of mud. Letsopa feela," she shook both her hands in the air with her big three-step gold wedding ring shining on her finger (mere clay). "But God saw it fit to bring us closer to Himself."

Someone tapped her shoulder and whispered something in her ear. She nodded before continuing.

"We will tell our children about it over and over. And if it takes Christmas to get the story of our Saviour heard, so be it," she paused and picked up her Bible from the table.

"Tshiamo, please read Matthew one, verses eighteen to twenty-five?"

A chubby teenage girl with thick and long relaxed hair stood up and began to read.

Most of the words went over Mmakoma's head. She wasn't paying much attention. She knew the story and it was becoming like a broken record. They repeated it so much in church that it became the reason why she just didn't go to church on Christmas.

"Behold, the virgin shall conceive and bear a son, and they shall call his name Immanuel, which means, God with us..."

Mavis sang again, a little longer this time and people started to pray. Had Mmakoma known that she was signing up for a church service, she would have declined the invitation. Not that there was anything wrong with church. She also went to church sometimes. It was the idea of being bamboozled into a service unawares that she didn't like.

She kept her eyes closed, saying no words to God. She listened to some of the people's passionate prayers. There was a feminine voice that prayed so fervently that she started to feel like a flood of water was washing over her own chest area. A flushing that her inner man needed.

"Lord," Mmakoma whispered out of her silence. "I'm not perfect but I'm your child. It's really nice to feel You like this. Please make it happen more often. I'd like to know you like she knows you."

Eventually less and less people were praying, until everyone was done, and Mrs Kgopa concluded by saying amen.

A man dressed in a white t-shirt and jeans went up to host the program.

"That's Moses," Boikarabelo said. "He's my cousin."

Mmakoma nodded. She wasn't really interested

but she supposed it made good conversation.

"Over there is his girlfriend, Busi and their son," she pointed at a full-figured woman with jeans and a white shirt. It was nice to see that most people had made the effort to stick to the theme. Her being in theme was a matter of pure coincidence. She always wore blue denim bottoms and a white top on Christmas, no matter where she was.

"That one over there with Kamano is Atang, my second eldest brother. After him there's Khumo, he's not here," her face glazed talking about her brothers.

"Atang's wife is in the kitchen. I'll introduce you to all the ladies," Boikarabelo went on.

"Let me first show you where the bathroom is," she led her into the house. It was a three bedroom that was nowhere near spacious. The dark brown sofas filled the living room, leaving little to no moving space. Then there was a dining area behind and a door to the kitchen ahead. Voices of ladies talking and laughing loudly were audible from where they were.

Mmakoma locked the door and relaxed to ease herself. But there was a knock on the bathroom door while she was in the middle of it.

"Someone," she said clumsily. No one could ever get used to someone else knocking in the midst of releasing number two, ever. To make it worse, the person waited on the passage. She walked out into a set of eyes that startled at her.

"You," it was Kamano with a silly smug on his face. Mmakoma wanted to bury her own face. She pulled her lip at him and walked towards the basin next door to wash her hands.

The festivities outside were gaining momentum and the dancing went on into the evening. It was getting more fun with the hours passing but Kamano was nowhere near. He was jumping up and down with the children, giving them snacks and making sure that they played safely. Not that Mmakoma minded it, the guy was annoying.

When it was getting dark, he dished up popcorn for the kids and began to set up for them to watch a movie. There was an argument until they all agreed on a movie.

The adults were outside in three groups. There was a group of the uncles, a group with the old aunties and a group of younger adults. The teens were all over the place, not too many of them and they were all on their phones.

"KK is always with the kids, look at him," someone said seeing Kamano talking to Tshiamo next to the braai stand.

"We should have gotten him Santa's costume," Atang laughed.

"Brother Kay," Maria called out. "Over here please."

"Ah, Maria, you summon me like your waiter in a

restaurant. I'm too expensive for that," Kamano said walking towards the place where they were sitting. He pulled his leg over the bench, and then the other and sat next to Tebogo.

"The kids have had enough of you. They want to have their own conversations without a forty-year-old in their midst," Maria said.

"I just wanted to make sure they don't gossip about me," Kamano said. "I had a mishap earlier and one of them saw it was me in there."

Everybody laughed.

"What did you do now buti?" Mercy, Atang's wife asked.

"Eish, my sister, ever had a situation where that one stool refused to go when you flushed?" he said playfully. They cringed.

"And a kid was waiting on the passage for me to finish, imagine," he opened his eyes wide, with his baritone adding to the humour. They laughed.

"I was there flushing, and the thing was not going anywhere," Kamano stood up and narrated with his hands. "I had to wait for the water to fill up again to make another attempt. The thing still didn't go. I had to wait again. The kid was knocking hysterically at this point. Akere he heard the flush, but uncle wasn't coming out."

"You should have told him to use the toilet outside," Maria laughed.

"*Hee*, there was no way I was exposing my voice. I

was hoping he would give up and leave," Kamano made his voice squeaky. They were all in tatters of laughter.

"Imagine these kids talking about their uncle like that. I have an image to protect. So, I was watching that kid closely and giving him that constant look to not even dare,"

"Whose kid was it? Atang asked.

"Ai, you're asking too many questions. Coming to think of it, I might be dehydrated. Bee, pass me some water please," Kamano said.

"Sure." Boikarabelo passed him a bottle of water from the bucket of drinks that was next to her.

The chatter and random moments of dancing went on till around 21h30. Kamano offered to drive Tebogo and Busi home. Boikarabelo asked him to take Mmakoma home too.

Mmakoma sat at the seat behind the driver's seat, Tebogo's son in the middle and Busi on the other side. Tebogo was the front passenger. The two of them in front carried the only conversation that was in the car until they reached Tebogo's place. The three of them got off and left Mmakoma and Kamano to drive off.

"For a moment I thought you were talking about me there," Mmakoma broke new silence in the car.

"Naa, my problems are bigger," he said, tilting the rear-view mirror to see her face.

"But I shouldn't have gone in there after you. Imagine your bomb plus my bomb and the kid thinking it's all my doing," Kamano said, sending Mmakoma into a howl of laughter.

"Oh well." She tried to compose herself.

"And I had the thought to use the outside toilet the minute I walked in after you. It was hard to breathe in there," he joked. Mmakoma laughed more.

Mmakoma gave her directions as he drove. She had eased into conversing with him.

He went out to open for her at the parking lot of her estate because his car doors still had child-lock set.

"I'd ask for the bathroom but we both know why it's best not to," he joked. She laughed gently before telling him about multiples of moments that were embarrassing when they happened but were now ridiculous and laughable. They conversed like old friends in the parking lot and time lapsed effortlessly. It was the chill of the very early hours of the next day that reminded him that he was supposed to be home, in bed already.

CHAPTER 6

"How's your friend?" Kamano asked pulling his feet that were covered in white socks up and resting them on the coffee table. Soccer practice had been physically demanding that evening.

"My friend?" Boikarabelo's puzzled face was visible to Kamano even though he wasn't looking at her directly.

"Yes. How's Doctor Komane?" He pressed the remote and switched to a soccer channel. A match between Manchester City and Real Madrid.

"Oh, she's fine. Why are you asking?"

"No reason."

"You've never asked about any of my friends.

Why her?"

"She's interesting. Different from all your other friends," he said passively.

"Different? Interesting? Or maybe you're just interested," she raised one of her brows.

"She's different in an interesting way," he maintained his laid-back demeanour.

"Oh?" Boikarabelo smiled dubiously.

"First, she's seven years older than you. None of your friends are that much older than you," he sat up straight, his eyes were still glued on the soccer match that was playing on screen. "Secondly, she's cheeky. All your other friends are typically nice people."

"She's also nice, I think," Boikarabelo.

"Not like you and your friends," he grinned, side-eyeing his younger sister.

"Oh okay." Boikarabelo considered the fact. "But how do you know she's seven years older than me?"

"I must have picked it up somewhere," Kamano moved into an upright sitting position. He was still wearing red sporting shorts and a red t-shirt from training. He had picked up soccer again after three years of avoiding the field.

"Didn't you mention her age at some point?" He gaslighted her. He had looked Mmakoma up online and amongst several other things he found out, was her date of birth. She was thirty-two years old.

He also knew that she was Dr Alice Komane's

daughter. The woman behind the most successful private clinic brand in Limpopo. Information about David Komane also came up during his search. He had never heard anything about him before. The man was behind the second largest black-owned construction company in the country, Komane Civils. A few articles also alluded to his partial ownership of a mining conglomerate.

"I don't think I've said anything about her age to you."

She stood up to go to the kitchen where Mavis, their mother was dishing up. Mavis was in there with Sally-Anne, Khumo's daughter. It would be a month before Khumo's return from Sudan, something that will grant Mavis much desired relief.

Having both Sally-Anne's parents actively serve in the military concerned her much. She enjoyed the brightening presence of a grandchild in her home every time both Khumo and Adilla got deployed out of the country, but it could never erase the fear of them never returning home. John left for work and never came back home twenty-five-years ago. She had envisioned a long and happy life with him, their children and their children's children. She sometimes wondered how her life would have been had John lived on.

Then God blessed her with Lesego, and she added three grandchildren to her family. But it was short-lived. She too left her house to watch Kamano play but never returned. With three of her grandchildren, she was gone for good.

Boikarabelo came back with a tray and two plates inside. She paused next to his feet that were stretched out and rested on the coffee table. Mavis hated that, and the mischief on Boikarabelo's face said it all. She was developing a disliking for it too.

"Please open the boom gate," she said sharply.

He moved one leg down, with a smirk on his face he moved the other. He held back his urge to laugh at her. He thought of telling her that it wasn't her house, but she still had his plate in her hands. It could all backfire for him, fast.

"Do you mind if I use your car to work tomorrow?" she asked him as he sat down.

He turned to look at her, then turned his face towards the television without replying.

"Buti, please. I'll pour petrol, I promise."

"Hee, you pouring petrol in my car? Where is my baby sister?" he laughed, and she also laughed. With the school being about two kilometres from Mavis' house, Kamano often walked to work.

"But you know what?" he had a sudden sparkle. "I'll drop you off and pick you up tomorrow."

"Thank you," Boikarabelo smiled relief. News had flown around town that there would be a protest of taxi and bus drivers the next day. If it was really happening, there would be no public transport to take her to work.

"You'll have to be up early," he said.

When they arrived at the hospital, Kamano watched Boikarabelo disappear into the hospital before getting off and trailing behind her. He felt like a naughty teenager for doing what he was doing.

"I'm looking for Dr Komane's rooms," he said to the receptionist. She was a woman in her forties with a welcoming face.

"You're early. She's here but she usually starts seeing people after 08h30," the woman touched her hair.

"You will go down that corridor, past the bathrooms. Look for 107," the lady explained, pointing in the direction with her hands. He thanked her and wasted no more time.

There were a few offices that belonged to other doctors on the corridor. He kept walking, reading every single door that he passed before seeing Dr MJ Komane, Cardiologist, Room 107. It was written in silver over the glass door. The walls inside were grey at the bottom and a wooden panel separated the upper part of the wall from the bottom. A purple, grey and bluish floral wallpaper decorated the upper part. There was also a large dark brown mahogany coffee table with magazines and flowers somewhere in the middle. The sofas were of brown leather that almost matched the mahogany table at the centre.

Kamano greeted the old lady who was sitting next to a child. On the other sofa was a couple in matching black t-shirts. A young child was playing in front of them. He smiled at them before facing the blonde-haired lady behind the information desk. She wore her hair in an asymmetrical bob and had the face of a thirty-something year old.

"Good morning sir," she greeted him first.

He didn't like the way she smiled. It seemed a little fake.

"Good morning. I'm here to see Dr Komane," he said.

"No problem Sir. Do you have a file with us?"

The blonde woman spoke with a subtle Afrikaans accent.

"No, I need to see her on a personal call," Kamano explained, looking around the room and softly tapping his shoe.

"I'll have to check with her first. You said your name is?"

"Kamano Kgopa," he said. Charlene began to write the name down on a sticky note. By the time she raised her head, Kamano was on his way to Mmakoma's office.

"No sir, please stop," she sprang off from her chair and paced behind him. "You don't have permission to see her already."

Kamano kept walking, ignoring whatever Charlene was saying behind him. Mmakoma's door wasn't closed, and it looked like she was alone. He knocked twice before letting himself in.

"Hi stranger," he smiled at her.

"I tried to stop him," Charlene appeared behind him, her red floral blouse and blue jeans seeming rather unorthodox for the hospital.

Mmakoma ran her eyes from Kamano to Charlene, "It's okay Charlene, thank you."

"You broke protocol," she moved her eyes back to him, and pushed part of her wig behind her right ear. It was dark brown hair that had a lighter shade at the tips which were just below her nape. She was wearing a cream white top that seemed to have been tailored for her body. It had a long zip at the back and the material of her formal trousers matched that of the top.

"That sounds a lot like me," he laughed. "How are you?"

"I'm okay. You?"

"I can be a lot better if I see the good doctor for lunch today."

"Are you asking me out Kamano?"

"No, I'm bringing you lunch. Unless if that's what you want to call it."

"Cool," she whispered with a wrinkle forming between her eyes.

"Great then, I'll see you at lunch time." He raised his thumb before he walked out. It left Mmakoma smiling.

Lunchtime, Kamano was there with a brown paper bag on his left and a paper tray that supported two cups of coffee on his right.

"I prefer tea," Mmakoma said opening the black lid over the paper cup to peruse. "But coffee will do for today. Thanks."

"You're welcome," Kamano said taking a seat. Mmakoma noticed the same navy-blue shirt he wore the first time she saw him. It looked better this time without that red jersey. Otherwise he would have looked like Postman Piet. He wore some old-looking grey chinos that looked like they had been ironed by an expert, with sharp creased straight lines in the middle of both legs (motshetshe).

"Don't you have clothes," she vocalised her thoughts.

"Well, I'm not naked. Or am I?" he joked, checking himself out.

"But…," she stopped herself. "Never mind."

"No problem."

He bit his sandwich and slowly lifted his eyes to catch her staring at him. She was waiting for the cue to eat.

"Bona petit." He swallowed uncomfortably.

"Thank you." She lifted her eyelids before starting to eat.

"You're welcome Miss Etiquette. Next time you'll remain hungry waiting for my permission to start eating." He pulled a deep infectious laughter.

Mmakoma laughed at herself. The conversation with Kamano left her cheered up into the rest of the afternoon.

He had offered to 'feed' her again the next day and she graciously accepted.

She asked Charlene to clear up a full hour for lunch the following day. Kamano's company, even just a little bit of it, left her refreshed.

That evening after work was scheduled for dinner with her father. She drove into traffic as she left the hospital. He had sent her the address of the restaurant. Her dad always did that. She wondered how he knew so many of these houses that no one else but the politicians and the wealthy seemed to know. From outside, you'd think that the place was just someone's house. Today's was a white house with a beautiful garden, nothing inviting and no board nor form of signage except for the house number. It was private and exclusive. The food was amongst the tastiest.

There was a lady who showed her where to park. Then she directed her to her father's table. He rose up to hug her and he shared a joke with the woman.

Although her old man was in construction, he never missed an opportunity to be in a suit and tie.

"I'm well dad. How are you?"

"Perfectly healthy. At my age, that's what matters."

"How did it go?" her father asked about a

meeting she had attended for Komane Civils earlier that week. It had been months since they'd sat together for dinner and David Komane wanted to get business matters out of the way first.

"We are looking at of four hundred and fifty million rands dad. But we'd have to provide guarantees beforehand," she explained.

"That shouldn't be a problem. I'll talk to Desireë to work on it right away. We can't afford to delay such a big project," he said.

"Okay," she sipped her juice as the waiter approached them with food.

"How are Mogau and Dipuo doing?" he asked as he received his food and nodded gratitude towards the waiter.

"They are fine. They'll be coming back to me tonight from the Makwela's," she said. Her father sighed before facing her with a blazing look.

"Is this the kind of family you want?" he said.

"What do you mean?"

"Children being tossed back and forth?" he elaborated.

"Dad, Lekau has made his decision, I'm okay with it. Please let it go," she said.

"If you insist my dear. But if you must know, this problem can be solved. You and Makwela's son can have a proper family, not this," he shook his hand in the air. Mmakoma had no doubt that her father could make things happen for her. If she said the word, he would move things around and she and Lekau would be in one home playing house next week.

There was a time when David pressed for a course of action, but her shame weighed on her like a heavy blanket. Her father's attempts to force the Makwela's to take responsibility would have made it worse. She was relieved that he, for once listened to her when she begged him not to act.

"*Dishonourable cowards*," Mmakoma remembered how her father spat those words in fury as he succumbed to her plea not to do anything about the matter.

It hurt her that Lekau was so quick to commit to Mmathapelo, but she also didn't want to be with a man who didn't choose her. It would have hurt more to wake up next to Lekau knowing that the only reason he was there was because her father pulled some strings and placed him and his family in a tight space. She also knew that the only reason her father hasn't shown hostility towards the Makwela's was not for the sake of their business dealings. It was for her sake. Had it been completely up to him, he would have burned bridges as soon as they found out that Lekau had had a wedding.

She had cried so much that evening. Her hopes to give her daughters a secure and stable family were out of the window, for good. Lekau never even bothered to extend the decency of an invitation, let alone a heads up. She had to hear it from the kids. She still chuckled in disbelief pondering over his audacity to have her daughters at a wedding that she knew nothing about.

"The longer you stay undecided, the harder it is for me to act," David Komane said.

"The decision is made dad. I'm over him," she said.

"You young ones miss the mark. Family is much more important than being infatuated with someone." David put a napkin over his neck as he held a fork and a knife.

"Makwela knows it. We would have talked it out as elders and convinced Lekau to treat you honourably. He can't just give you two children and run to marry someone else."

Mmakoma hid her mouth behind her glass and mumbled, "Dad, I don't want to be with someone who's not in love with me."

David looked at her tenderly and said nothing. She wondered what he would have said if he had known about Nat. David Komane was a softie when it came to her, but he was still rigid and old-fashioned to the core.

CHAPTER 7

"How were your holidays girls?" Mmakoma asked offhandedly with much of her attention given to her screen.

"It was so fun. My favourite part was playing with our little brother, Papi," Dipuo said.

"Your little brother?" Mmakoma clicked to save her spreadsheet before gazing at Dipuo. A hot tingling reached parts of her face. Lekau was doing it again. First it was having to hear from the kids that he had a wedding, now it was a hidden baby. She forced a smile towards Dipuo before moving it towards Mogau who was at the fridge with a tub of ice-cream.

"You Mogau? How were your holidays?" she diverged.

"It was nice mommy, Mmathapelo was nice. She played with us sometimes, and she let us eat nice things," Mogau said.

"That much I can tell. Look at how much weight you've gained," Mmakoma said sharply.

Mogau looked at herself and her face fell flat.

"Don't be like that, I'm helping you. No one likes fat people," Mmakoma said.

"Eat, you already have it in a cup." Mmakoma snapped noticing the change on Mogau's face.

She restrained herself from lashing more words towards her. Mogau struggled to swallow in the icecream with her mother's eyes on her. Khabonina passed behind and brushed her shoulder lightly. Mmakoma went back to her computer screen pretending to have not noticed Khabonina give her daughter a touch of comfort.

It was now routine for Kamano to come into Mmakoma's place of work with food.

"People will start thinking that you're the delivery man," she joked as he came into her office.

"Dr Komane," that was his way of greeting her.

"It doesn't sit well every time you call me Dr Komane," she closed one of her patient's files.

"Why?"

"Something in the way you say it makes me

wonder if that's all there is to me," she stood up with her blue scrubs to put the file with others in her cabinet.

"Having the title is a badge of honour. You must wear it with pride."

He sat down and placed two salad containers on the table. He had a royal blue soccer gear on.

"Why are you dressed this way? Don't you have decent clothes?" she asked.

"You want me to start dressing up to come here? Is it a job now?"

"Mara, Kamano, a matching soccer gear?" she searched for something in his eyes.

"You're in your doctor's gear, I'm in my soccer gear, what's wrong?" he chewed some fruit nonchalantly, unfazed by her gaze.

"But if you must know, I'm on my way to Mahwelereng for a soccer match," he explained. "And you? Why aren't you in your ordinary clothes?"

"Ordinary clothes? Those are designers," she giggled.

"Oh," he folded his arms. "Why aren't you in your designers?"

"I am going to theatre," she said.

"I see," he picked a block of pawpaw from his container with a fork and chewed. His jawline moved sharply. Mmakoma noticed it.

"I have to go now," he looked at her.

"Mahwelereng Stadium is about an hour from here."

"All the best with that," she stood up and walked him out. He shared a hilarious story of something that happened between him and one of his brothers before leaving. Mmakoma walked him out to the front desk of her practice. He waved goodbye to Charlene.

"He's nice," she said behind him.

"Oh, please Charlene, he's not my type," Mmakoma rolled her eyes.

"And your type is?" Charlene's hair fell over her eye, she fixed it with her hand.

"I'm not that sure anymore. I've kissed enough frogs in my life," Mmakoma laughed.

"I like this one for you," Charlene.

"No thank you. I don't want another Nat in my life. I mean the guy is just a school principal who still stays with his mother at forty."

"Ooh, that's bad," Charlene laughed. "At least he makes a decent living and is not a lazy trust fund baby."

"But you know my circles. You know my parents. I wouldn't be able to take him anywhere."

"Who said you needed to take him anywhere? A little fooling around wouldn't hurt anyone."

Charlene pulled her lip before applying pink lipstick.

"I don't know if I still want to play. My girls will be teens in a few years. I can't be playing while they are also playing," Mmakoma laughed at the thought as she moved around the front desk to check her diary that Charlene kept.

"I told you about Rhulani right?"

"The one who is a doctor?"

"He's been sending me messages. Guy wants to play again," Mmakoma pulled breath. "He says he'll be passing Polokwane on his way to Elim."

"That one sounded like a catch." Charlene was excited.

"My appetite for games is gone Charlene. All gone," Mmakoma said, browsing her schedule for the coming week.

She made mental notes before walking to her office to grab a few things and off to theatre she went.

She came back with bloodshot eyes, "Please don't allow any walk-ins."

She sped past Charlene without a care for her response. Charlene knew the look; she knew what it meant. She shook her hands in the air as she rushed to close the doors to the practice.

On the other side, Mmakoma pushed her office door feeling her strength deplete. She let herself to the floor and a piercing lament went out of her vocal cords.

"Why?" she wailed.

"Why?" she wailed again with a bumpy rhythm accompanying her words.

Uncontrolled streams rolled down her face and her nostrils also produced. She threw her face between her knees and tried to breathe through her congested nose.

More mucus came out and more tears came out. She pulled a hand towel from the holder on the wall behind her and wiped her face before blowing her nose. A hollow feeling had taken over her inner parts. Her wall gave testament to her hard work and achievements but her failure to save that two-year-old boy spoke louder in her soul.

The boy grew faint in her care. He lost his battle for life gradually. She was losing hers too. His father was outside. He expected a hopeful answer. He had paid with everything he had to get the boy treated.

It wasn't her battle. She kept reminding herself. Her inner parts spoke contrarily. She felt every part of it. She grieved the death of the innocent child like it was her own. Her heart was torn. She touched the baby's face and whispered some words. He was gone. His body was frozen and lifeless.

She invited the parents into a counselling room that was next to where the ward nurses sat.

"Mr and Mrs Mangena, I'm afraid to say this. Your son is no longer with us."

"My babyyyyyy," Mrs Mangena wailed in devastating sorrow. Mr Mangena's eyes turned red. He held his wife who was now struggling to maintain form. Mmakoma felt her walls break down.

The experience was now her own and she was tearing up. She walked out of the room and instructed the senior nurse to see to the family.

"She's not in good shape," Charlene explained to Kamano as he walked in a few minutes after.

"I'll be brief."

He ignored Charlene's gatekeeping like he always did. She made no effort to stop him. She was at the verge of crying herself. Mmakoma's lament had been heart-wrenching to listen to. She had shut her eyes in distress with every sound of it.

"I said no one," Mmakoma shouted at hearing a knock on her closed office door.

The person opened anyway. She was still on the floor with thick and puffy eyes. She raised her head to find Kamano's face and then she dropped it again.

Kamano placed the bag of food on the table and closed the door. He sat next to her on the floor.

"My life is meaningless." Her voice was breaking. "I took a vow to save lives, to heal people, to help people live. I couldn't do it today."

"It wasn't you." Kamano touched her hand that weightlessly rested on her thigh.

"No Kamano, it was me, all me." She dropped her head. "Nothing I touch lives."

Kamano squeezed her hand gently and said

nothing. She breathed hard.

"That mother's cry Kamano," Mmakoma sniffed.

"God will comfort her," Kamano said.

"I shouldn't be a doctor. Nothing I touch lives," she sobbed.

"Don't say that," Kamano said.

"The other day I told my daughter that she was fat. I saw her die inside. I've become my mother," she cried.

"Death surrounds me, and I'm the creator of it. I vowed to stop it, but I fail all the time Kamano. All the time."

"Your name comes highly recommended. If what you are saying is true, you wouldn't be the cardiologists you are," he reassured her.

"The first person to die in my hands was Aunty Tsakani. The only person in this world who genuinely cared about me," she sniffed and wiped her mucus with her hand.

Kamano got up to get her some tissue from her table.

"Thank you," she said as she began to blow her nose with pink tissue.

"Then it was my own child. My flesh and blood. I never gave that baby a chance to be a human being in this world. I still wonder if it would have been a boy or a girl," she said.

Kamano was now the third person living to know this. It was something that only Lekau and Nathaniel knew. And now Nathaniel was gone. He had followed his child to wherever dead souls went.

"Don't be so hard on yourself." He touched her shoulder.

"I'm a failure at saving lives. Who am I fooling here?" Her words were followed by prolonged silence.

"Doc." Kamano's hand moved on top of hers.

"All these lives you are talking about, you never gave them in the first place. The choice to let people die or live has never been yours. You only know about life and healing just enough to be a tool in God's hand. That's all."

Mmakoma shifted to straighten herself. The floor was getting cold. Her bum was beginning to feel the floor's hardness.

"I must be a useless tool then," she moaned.

"You know it's not true," Kamano.

"Let me tell you something," Kamano spoke again. "For almost three years, I lived like a dead man. My wife, Lesego and my three kids all died in a car accident coming to watch me play. I carried the guilt and I lived with it. I embraced it. She was such a good person, why didn't God take me instead? Why didn't I leave with them earlier? Why did I invite them to my game? Those questions haunted me."

Mmakoma turned to face him.

"I left home that morning without telling her that

I loved her. I didn't even kiss nor hug my kids. I just hurried to a match. All this made me feel like I killed them," he breathed.

"But here's the thing. I am no saviour, I'm not God. Some things in life are not within my control."

"How can you say that when your wife and kids are gone?" There was a puzzle in Mmakoma face.

"If you spoke to me a year ago, I would have never said that. But I realised that the weight of thinking that saving my wife and my children's lives was something within my power created a prison for me," he said.

His bum was starting to hurt from the floor too. Mmakoma stood up to go and sit on her chair. He also stood up to take a seat.

"Where was I when God created Lesego? Where was I when God created all the sperm cells within my body?" he laughed a bit. "You doctors say there's about one million of them in a teaspoon, right?"

"Yes," Mmakoma blushed, and a dry smile formed on her face.

"Imagine, every day, one million unique people from my loins posing before Lesego's egg," he chuckled.

"One million every day?" Mmakoma cracked up in laughter.

"Some days it would be two million, or three," he said.

"Don't look at me like that, I had a good marriage." Mmakoma snorted in laughter.

"All this to say, there is a Saviour who knows much more about life and saving lives. He is not confined to life as we see it here. If we help people, we are just a tool in His hand. We are not Him," he said.

"And what about the kind of death we could have prevented?"

"Look, I don't know everything. All I know is that I thought I knew God well. Then my wife died, and I lived in guilt and bitterness. I thought feeling like that was a way of recompense. I thought I deserved the pain for all the wrongs I've done. But all that was rebellion. A sneaky kind of rebellion."

"Why would you call carrying guilt rebellion?"

"How do you explain me being ruled by guilt when Christ freely hung on the cross for me?"

"I'm lost Kamano. My doctor brain likes things broken down to the cell," she said.

"Good thing I'm a teacher," he smiled.

"Look," he said. "The reason Christ died on the cross when he was sinless was to carry our guilt. To take the sentence in our place. The wages of sin are death. He took the death on our behalf."

"Okay," Mmakoma tilted her head and clipped her chin with her folded pointy finger and thumb.

"When I embrace guilt and continue to put myself in guilty situations, I literally dishonour His death.

It's like I am saying that His sacrifice means nothing to me," Kamano said.

"I don't think that's right," she said. "We feel guilty because we are remorseful."

"But it mustn't end at feeling remorseful. It's important to say, I'm sorry, I'll never do it again. Then you do everything in your power not to do it again," Kamano added.

"And here's the thing," he looked at her. "When Jesus grants you freedom to live like you never did anything wrong, but you insist on living like you did, it shows that you missed the point of his sacrifice."

Mmakoma removed her face from Kamano and looked at her clutched hands on the table. She fiddled them a bit, "The boy's parents had hope that I would save their son."

"He was only two years old Kamano. Just two. Why does God allow such? Why?"

Kamano's eyes met hers. She wanted him to say something.

"Mmakoma," he called her by her name for the first time. His melodious baritone reached for something deep in her. Mmakoma was the name her late grandmother gave her.

"God allows so many things to happen, good and bad."

He touched her clutched hands with both his.

CHAPTER 8

Mmakoma drove into the home she grew up in. It was a cream and grey house with four bedrooms that all had en-suite bathrooms. Only a few things had changed since her childhood, the paint being the most obvious deviation from the white house that she grew up in.

Alice and David had two other houses in Polokwane, one in Johannesburg and another in Bloemfontein. David Komane preferred to spend his days in Polokwane at the house in Bendor while Alice Komane loved being in Hospital Park. It made sense for any doctor to stay in the area anyway.

The construction business still kept David

Komane on the road even though he had slowed down his travels with the years.

Mmakoma parked her 4Matic behind a dark grey Renault Megane. The car had a bump and some scratches on the side. It was not new to her eye, and she tried to recollect where she could have seen it. Her memory failed her.

The wooden double door that served as a front door wasn't locked. It never occurred to her to knock first. Something Alice had reprimanded her over a million times for. It just never came naturally to do so at a place so familiar to her. Personally, she wasn't the type to lock doors. It just made life hard to navigate. She sometimes forgot that other people preferred it differently.

"Name the price." She heard her mother say.

"My baby's life is not for sale. Sorry Alice."

It was a familiar voice responding. Mmakoma held her feet steadily at the entrance hall. She thought of walking back to knock, or maybe even leave. But if she left, her mother would know from CCTV that she had been there.

"You are in my court right now little girl. I can finish you and no one will know what happened to you," her mother said.

She could hear them clearly from the other side of the display wall at the entrance. There was a stand with some souvenirs and a vase.

"Isn't five hundred thousand or maybe six

hundred thousand rands enough to keep your mouth shut and disappear from our lives for good?"

"Come on Alice. You want me to disappear for life here. I will be raising this baby on my own, not bothering you and David. What's six hundred thousand rands?"

"How much do you want? A million?" Alice asked. Mmakoma tiptoed back to the door to knock.

Alice opened and hugged her. She was in a loose pink summer dress.

"I've got a guest, but you can come in. She was about to leave." Alice led Mmakoma to the living room.

Mmakoma blinked twice when she saw the familiar face. She had met her once at Cindy's birthday party.

"Hi," the lady greeted her casually. She seemed neither surprised nor shocked.

Mmakoma couldn't utter any words to greet back. Her mouth was dry. Her name was Naledi.

"I was here to see your mom. We are done."

She was leaving. Her small bump was visible in that brown dress with buttons from the top to the bottom. Her weave was Peruvian, Mmakoma could tell from just looking at it.

"You've put on centimetres," Alice said to Mmakoma while pressing a button to let Naledi out.

Mmakoma touched her own waist and smoothed down to her hips. It must be from Kamano's food.

"Leticia's daughter is getting married in two months. You need to be in shape for that wedding," Alice said.

"Leticia?"

"Yes, Leticia Mokoena-Anderson."

"Isn't that invitation just for you mom?"

"This is one wedding you cannot afford to miss Mmakoma," Dr Alice Komane said.

"Hew mom, I don't even know Aunt Leticia's daughter that well."

"Exactly why you need to be in that room. How do you think we built everything we have?" Alice sat down on the leather sofa adjacent to the one Mmakoma was sitting on.

"I don't know mom." She pulled breath.

"Relationships with the right people are very important, Janet. You need to be in the right places to meet right people."

Alice's red lipstick brightly accentuated her lips against her sun-kissed matured yellowish skin. Her hair was a short s-curl.

"I'll think about it. I don't want to look like a fool whose name is nowhere on the guest list," Mmakoma said.

"Oh, your name will be on that guest list. Trust me," Alice said.

It wasn't too long before she left her mother's house for Cindy's apartment. Something about Naledi didn't sit well with her and she wasn't going to go to bed with the discomfort.

"Your friend, Naledi..." she paused to study Cindy's face. "Whose child is she carrying?" she didn't mince her words in interrogation. It made Cindy shiver nervously.

"MJ," Cindy's cheeks flushed up.

"Answer my question." Impatience vibrated through Mmakoma's voice.

"I didn't think anything would come out from it. I really didn't."

Cindy started fidgeting. The teaspoon in her hands was shaking.

"What do you even mean Cindy? What nonsense is this?" Mmakoma.

"She was looking for work for her company, I connected her with your dad," she paused. "My friend is into older men. That's how she finances her lavish Instagram life. I just didn't think she would go for your dad."

"Is that all?"

"Yes, that's the whole truth friend."

"I don't even know how to feel about this. I don't."

"I'm sorry friend."

"No, you're not. You're doing exactly the same thing with someone else's father right now." Mmakoma was sharp in the tongue. It wasn't in her to beat about the bush.

"Don't judge me MJ. You have no idea how it

feels to have your rich parents suddenly become bankrupt. You have no idea," Cinderella said. Mmakoma kept a stern face. She was unmoved.

"You're a doctor, you'll never have to be in my position," Cinderella said.

"Pshht, whatever Cindy."

Mmakoma was fuming. She turned around and went for the door.

She found Khabonina tucking Dipuo to sleep. She kissed her forehead, then she touched Mogau's gentle face. She was fast asleep.

She walked to the kitchen for a bottle of red wine and poured herself a glass before catching some fresh air from her balcony.

CHAPTER 9

Muzi sat on the chair across Mmakoma's desk and began to talk about the Mokoena-Anderson wedding as his perfume slowly took over the airspace around him.

"Sounds like you need a plus one." Mmakoma cut his long musings short. If left uninterrupted, he could go on and on forever.

"You can say that," he said diplomatically clearing his throat. Mmakoma refrained from rolling her eyes. She yawned instead.

"I'll think about it and let you know," she said. Muzi was a man of far-reaching influence but she had been around him often enough to not see him the same way distant admirers did.

"I've got a lot of work to run over right now," she dismissed him.

He got the hint and got up. Mmakoma hid the amusement she felt at him getting it so quickly. It was in his nature to prolong conversations just to talk about himself and to also drop some big names.

"Well then, I'll hear from you." He tucked his white shirt into his navy formal trousers before opening the door.

It became wild when Kamano appeared on the other side with a fist that was ready to knock. Muzi startled at him, and he returned the look with the same passion and intensity.

"Heita." Kamano finally stepped aside to let Muzi pass.

Muzi ran his eyes from Kamano's head to toes and back up. It was a condescending look that Mmakoma picked up. It became weirder when Muzi's eyes moved up again to find Kamano's waiting blazingly for him. His usual friendly face was now replaced by a rigid challenging look.

"Sure," Muzi responded in confident egotism before walking away. Kamano looked at his back briefly. He must have lashed out a few swear words in his head.

"Who's that?" he asked.

"Just a guy I know," Mmakoma said casually.

"I don't like him."

"It didn't look like he liked you either," Mmakoma joked. Kamano didn't laugh.

She went around her table and sat down to face his direction.

"I'm going to a wedding with him in three weeks." She opened the meal pack that Kamano had just placed on the table before he even offered. He was in clean discoloured straight-leg jeans with a geometric crease in the middle of both legs. It vexed her but she decided to keep her thoughts to herself.

"Hm, you're going to the wedding with him," he repeated her words to himself in a low tone. He touched his food container but did not remove the seal on it.

"You can go with me," he said, his eyes still set on the food.

"Naa, you wouldn't fit in," Mmakoma replied casually. Kamano allowed the subtle sounds of Mmakoma chewing to be the only thing audible.

Then he breathed in and out heavily.

"Let me tell you something now," he said. "I'm trying to get into your life. Thought I would do this slow and gradual, but it looks like I will need to be more direct."

Mmakoma raised her brows in surprise. She still had a chip in her hand and some food in her mouth.

"I'm not here to just be the clown. I'm here to be your man," Kamano said.

She laughed. He didn't.

"Kamano," she calmed her laughter. "I like you as a person. I love being around you. But you are not my type."

"Of course, I'm not your type. I'm unlike any of those in that category. I am the final stop."

He was no longer looking at the food. He was fixed on her. Right into her eyes.

"What are you saying? I thought we were just friends."

"I'm okay with being your friend but I'm also trying to get to know you."

"That's fine," she said.

"I don't think so," he continued. "What I'm saying is, I'd like to get to know you as a man does the woman he loves."

Mmakoma stopped. She moved in her seat to comprehend. She hadn't expected it.

"Whoa, Kamano." She shook her head. "That's a bit too much for me."

"I'm not expecting anything from you other than you considering it," he said.

"Okay." A wrinkle formed on her forehead. Kamano covered his untouched food and got up from his chair.

"I will see you again soon." His eyes went deep into hers, then he walked out.

Mmakoma breathed hard. Kamano wasn't quite the type of man she would pick in a crowd and it wasn't his physique that would make her pass over him because he had the body of a fit rugby player that was wasted in old geometrically ironed trousers. He just didn't know how to dress for it, and he didn't care to change.

The one thing she always noticed in a man was his shoes, then his perfume if he got close enough, then it would be how he dressed and how well-groomed he was. The only thing about Kamano that made it into that criteria was grooming.

That Saturday, Mmakoma visited her mother. Patrick Zimba's double cab was driving out when she arrived. She pulled her hand out and waved at him, but he seemed reluctant to wave back. He didn't even say a word. It was unlike him. The timer always wanted to talk. That's how she's known him for the twenty years he has been with Komane Civils.

Mmakoma found Alice in her kitchen making food. This was something she almost never did when she was growing up. There was always someone else to cook meals, never Alice. Mmakoma had no memory of it. Not even one when her mother packed her lunch for school, or made her a bowl of cornflakes, nothing.

"Hi mom." She sat on the brown kitchen stool.

"Hi Janet," Alice said filling still water into a glass. She studied the floral top her daughter was wearing. Then she looked at her jeans and lastly threw a look at her sandals.

"What was Mr Zimba here for?" Mmakoma asked curiously.

"Mr Zimba?" The question threw Alice off.

"Yes. What was he here for? I greeted him and he didn't stop to chat," Mmakoma said in dry and brief humour.

She and her father always joked about how the man never stopped talking.

"He must have been in a hurry. I asked him to come and check the taps." Alice looked away and started to rub the roses that were in a vase next to her cookbooks.

"You said you wanted to see me ASAP." Mmakoma relaxed on her chair. The house felt emptier than it did when she was growing up. There were always servants working inside and outside but now her mother only had temporary helpers that came on specific days of the week.

"Yes, the Mokoena-Anderson wedding is in two weeks," Alice said.

Mmakoma brushed her hand against the other and waited for her mother to say more.

"Do you have an outfit?" It was like her to check on her daughter's perfection before an important event.

"I'll find something. The theme is black and white right?"

The little bit of investment she had towards the event was to please Alice and not from any genuine interest. She didn't know Aunt Leticia's daughter enough to be excited in any type of way.

"Yes, it's black and white. You have to look the part Janet. Make a plan, quickly." Alice lightly banged the glass of water against the countertop.

The way she looked at it showed that she hadn't expected it to hit as hard as it did. "I still need to see the outfit you decide on and give it a thumbs up, or down. We don't have a lot of time Janet."

Janet was the name Alice gave her. Mmakoma was given by her father's mother, after her late aunt. Alice preferred Janet over Mmakoma. She said the name was backwards and she didn't even like the aunt that her daughter was named after.

"I'm on it mom," Mmakoma said.

"You had better be."

"I will be."

"Your plus one?" Alice raised her face for an answer.

"You mom. I can go with you," Mmakoma sneered.

"No, I'm going with Daddy. He'll be around for the wedding," Alice said. Mmakoma wanted to ask how she convinced him this time.

"I'll find someone."

She picked a grape from a bowl on the counter. Alice stopped, then continued chopping a carrot from a brown wooden board.

Mmakoma didn't want to mention Muzi because it would encourage her. The next best thing to arriving with a famous politician's famous son was to be seen with the son of the president himself.

"You only have a week Janet. One week." Alice wiped her hands and grabbed a notebook that was next to the cookbooks. She wrote something on it.

"I think we have run over all the important things," She closed her notebook letting Mmakoma feel some relief at being expected to fulfil two things only. A date and an outfit. Alice's lists had been exhaustive before.

She asked to be excused, leaving Alice to continue making a lunch of salmon and vegetables.

Cinderella had called the night before. She sounded distraught over the phone. Things hadn't been the same since their fight over Naledi, but she still cared.

When she arrived at Cindy's place, she hugged her friend like nothing ever happened between them.

"MJ, I'm sorry about last time," she poured her some wine.

"I'm also sorry. I shouldn't have blamed you for Naledi's..." Mmakoma paused to think of a more suitable word.

"It's water under the bridge," Cindy said, picking

up a pink fleece that fell on the floor when she went to open for Mmakoma. The weather was beginning to feel chilly indoors even though the outdoors were still sunny. Mmakoma sat on the black L-shaped leather sofa and placed her glass on the table. She slid her feet off her sandals and rested her back.

"Please don't come at me for mentioning her name. I know the pain she has caused, but I'm worried." Cindy put her hand over her cheek.

"What now?" Mmakoma said.

"I got a call from Naledi's cousin two days ago. Apparently, she unexpectedly left. She called them to say she'll be away for some time. She said she'll be fine and that they mustn't worry about her," Cindy explained.

"That's strange."

"Very."

Cindy put her wine glass over the table and faced her friend who could have been estranged by now, but it was unlikely. Theirs was a friendship that survived fights and distance over the years.

"To make matters worse, she's not active on all her social media accounts. It's unlike her."

"I know you care about her, but I want nothing to do with that girl," Mmakoma.

"And rightly so."

Cindy put her glass down and ran her long pink nails through her long weave. The bottom part of her tailored red dress remained hidden under her fleece as she gazed at Mmakoma with pleading eyes.

"Her family is really worried, and they don't know who the father of that baby is."

"Why are you telling me all of this?" Mmakoma closed her eyes and shook her head in disbelief.

"You know people, and I know I can trust you. Why don't you make calls? Perhaps someone can track her down."

"No Cindy, that's a long stretch," Mmakoma said. "And I'd rather not be involved in all this."

"Please my friend. Please, it's your half sibling she's carrying," Cindy pleaded.

The possibility of a sibling hit Mmakoma for the first time. It made her inner parts tremble. It made it all real.

Her childhood days were spent with a longing for a brother or sister. She missed Jackson, her twin brother. Even though he died when they were still four-year-old toddlers, her heart always felt his room and his absence. A faint memory of him still resided her mind. Alice always shut off any discussion of his death. It was a taboo topic for the Komane's.

"I don't know Cindy, I don't know."

She tenderly rubbed her neck and pulled the skin around it forward. With the same hand, she covered that neck.

"At least think about it. I am really worried about her."

Mmakoma wanted to say something, but her

phone rang. It was a number she had never seen before.

"Hello," she reluctantly answered.

"Doc…" It was Kamano.

This was the first time ever that Kamano called her. It was odd that they had never exchanged numbers after months of sharing food.

"Kamano, hi."

"I happen to know that you're not working today." He sounded happy.

This was the Kamano she liked, not the jealous version she saw last.

"You went to the hospital?" she laughed at him.

"Nope. I happen to have other ways of acquiring information," he said. "I will be playing at Peter Mokaba stadium this afternoon. It would be nice if you came through."

"Naa, soccer is not really my thing," Mmakoma said indifferently.

"You can come with the girls. They will love it." As if he didn't hear her.

"They never watch soccer."

"Are you home? I'm coming to pick you up now." He carried on like he wasn't registering her words.

"That's the thing. I'm not even home."

"Send me your location, I'm coming."

"Kamano…" she called his name.

"I'm cutting the call. Please send it." He hung up.

This was a lot like him, Charlene even gave up on trying to gatekeep him at the practice.

Please send, I'm waiting -A message came in on WhatsApp.

Mmakoma smiled at seeing soccer boots as his profile photo.

"Who was that?" Cindy.

"Just a guy I know." Mmakoma lifted her shoulders and fixed her floral top.

"Ooh." Cindy was getting excited.

"You even look uncomfortable trying to reduce him to just another guy."

"No Cindy," Mmakoma giggled. "He makes me laugh, that's all."

"Ooh, what does he do?" Cindy had a sparkle all over her face.

"He's a principal in Seshego," Mmakoma said.

"You never learn," Cindy's face changed.

"He also plays soccer."

Mmakoma felt a need to come to Kamano's defence and to build him up in her friend's eyes.

"He loves children." She desperately threw that in. Thinking of all the good things she could say came with an unexpected desire for his company. She hadn't thought about it before, but Kamano felt like a place of rest. There was never a need to pretend with him. She could fart and he would turn it into the most hilarious joke. She could just be. She wanted to tell her but realised it would sound like she admired him overly. She startled at her friend's disapproving face and loved how rebellious she felt.

I'm at Riverdale Boulevard, come get me. – she texted him back.

"He's coming to fetch me. I'm going to watch him play today," Mmakoma said. Cindy inhaled some air and looked at Mmakoma.

"Don't do it friend," she warned.

The more she warned her, the more she just desired to be with him. To share his company. To hear his jokes. To watch his jawline moving up and down while he chewed.

He was there in thirty minutes. Mmakoma walked down the staircases with her jeans, floral top and green Hermes Oran leather sandals, feeling like a sixteen-year-old about to do as she pleased. Cindy followed behind briskly spitting disapproving words. But she still had to see this school principal with her own eyes.

"I'll call to fetch my car." Mmakoma turned backwards to tell her friend and to wave at her. Her handbag flew in the air as she turned her body frivolously to keep walking forward.

"He drives a polo." Cindy was further disappointed. Mmakoma kept walking.

Kamano stepped out of the car. He already had a soccer kit on. His face blazed fervently as he smiled at her. This was the most relaxed he'd ever seen her. She was always careful with her image and somehow formally dressed.

The floral top made her ooze with femininity. Her weave was off, and her hair was in a puffed ponytail. He went around to open the door for her and greeted Cindy while at it.

The number of organisations that sponsored the tournament was the first thing Mmakoma noticed. The league was for players that were over the age of thirty-five. Although they received some sort of income from sponsorships, money wasn't their motivation. Proceeds of their games went into young talent in Seshego and in the villages around Polokwane. This was exactly what got Kamano playing in the league in the first place. It is what got him working hard again when it dawned on him that his life still lied ahead of him. He had lost it all buy he still had to live.

"I never thought I'd ever catch myself going to the stadium for a soccer match," Mmakoma said.

"There's a first time for everything," he said as he shut the car doors and began walking her towards the section where she was going to sit. There weren't too many people yet.

"Thank you for coming," he said, handing her a card.

"What's this?"

"VIP access," he said casually. "Enjoy the game."

He tenderly touched her hand as she received the card and then ran into what seemed to be changing rooms.

Mmakoma followed the usher's instructions that led her to the VIP area. She bought herself juice and popcorn on the way and went to sit down. It was a while before the match began but seeing Kamano run behind the ball made up for all the time she sat waiting. He was something else on the field.

CHAPTER 10

"My designer is coming tonight. Please come over for measurements," Mmakoma said over the phone. Kamano was taken aback.

"*Excuse me.*" He positioned himself.

"We've only got a few days to get outfits for the wedding."

"Oh," he jested in his baritone. "I'm going with you?"

"Please come over. We need these outfits as in yesterday," she said.

"Your designer must be a pain in the pocket." he said casually.

"It's Johnston Khaya. He does come a bit pricey," she confirmed his suspicion. "But don't worry about the cost, I'll cover it."

"No, I'll get myself a suit at the mall."

"No Kamano, I'll cover it. It's completely fine by me." Her breathing made it sound like she was walking, then suddenly stopped.

"Doc, I'm good."

No woman was going to pay for his clothes. More especially a woman of his interest.

"But he's already expecting…"

"I said I'm good," he insisted.

There was a knock on his office door. It must have been Palesa Morokane bringing another backchatting learner to the principal's office. Her lack of experience made her an easy target and she was yet to develop a thick skin with the learners.

"Please hold for a second," he said to Mmakoma.

It was Palesa indeed, with Thabo Maila. Kamano already knew why they came to his office.

"Doc let me attend to this. I'll give you a call later." He placed his phone face down on his table.

"Thabo Maila, you're in my office again," Kamano said.

"The girls are blowing this out of proportion, Sir. I was only joking," the boy said.

"Clearly it wasn't a joke to them," Kamano said. "Miss Morokane you may excuse us. This boy will be back in your classroom with a better attitude in no time."

Palesa Morokane nodded her head and turned to

walk away.

"Thabo, you cannot be in my office for the same thing over and over again."

"But sir…" the boy tried to protest.

"I should call your mother again."

"Please sir, don't call her," Thabo pleaded.

The threat to call his mother was a reminder of a possible humiliation. She was a woman given to much alcohol. She was the type that trembled if they hadn't had a sip. Being one of the boys who were trying to appear cool in school, he never wanted any of the other learners to see his mother. This, Kamano discovered last time he had called her in to discuss Thabo's disciplinary issues. Two learners walked into the office building as they were walking out. The boy swiftly moved into the female teachers' bathrooms just to avoid being seen with her. Kamano wanted to lash him for running into the female teachers' bathroom but the shame on his face when he came out was enough apology. It said it all.

"Our society cannot function without women, at all."

Kamano was sharp in the boy's eyes. He dropped his head.

"I know," he said.

"If you knew, you'd know better than to utter such harassment." The boy's eyes opened wide.

"They may not have the physical ability to wrestle you, but you are well-dressed and well-fed like this because of a woman. She stayed even when the tough man ran. You do not lack because that woman makes sure you don't. Is she perfect? No. But she does her best."

Thabo's eyes began to fill up.

"That woman was once a beautiful young girl, like the ones you mistreat now. It's up to you to be a better man. A man of honour. A man who is able to uphold a woman's honour."

Kamano was aware of how the departure of his father from their lives broke the boy's mother. She wasn't always the way that she now was. Millicent Maila used to be known for her beauty in Seshego. She even held the Miss Seshego title at some point. Dozens of men used to drool over her. Amongst them, she chose the one who was more in love with her looks than her personhood. His name was Victor Makwarela, a talented musician who attracted the attention of many ladies. They became the most coveted couple of their time. The tag, couple goals was not yet a thing, but had it been, it would have been a perfect description for them. Kamano was a few years younger than Millicent, but it was well-known that that was how she ended up with the bottle in her mouth. That was probably the only version of Millicent that the boy came to know as a mother, broken and forsaken.

"You must challenge yourself to be a better man." Kamano gazed into the boy's teary eyes. "I'll be watching you for the next three months. I must never hear a single complaint from any teacher or learner about you. Nothing at all."

"Okay sir," Thabo nodded.

"I will also be watching your performance closely. So, you better pull those socks up, boy."

"Challenge accepted, Sir."

He shyly wiped his eyes with his shirt and stood up.

"See you on the other end of the challenge." Kamano stood up from his table.

The boy left his office and closed the door on his way out. He sat down. Then he heard a screeching sound from his phone. He picked it to check.

"*Ye* Doc, you've become the paparazzi now," he said playfully.

"The storyline was so juicy, I couldn't hang up," she said. But the reason she never gave him was that she heard a female voice in the beginning and became curious.

"Ehm, to pick up where we left off, may I at least go with you when you go shopping for your suit?" By her judgement so far, Kamano wasn't the most stylish of the lot. In fact, he seemed to care very little about what he was wearing. If she was to appear at a high-profiled wedding with him, she was going to see to it that he looked his best.

With his arm rested over his fully open window, Mmakoma caught his eye as she walked towards him at the parking lot. She had a tailored cream dress with her beige Chanel pumps that had a black seal in front. Her scent was heavenly as she opened the door and sat inside. His eyes had been too captivated to remember to get out and open the door like he promised himself to.

No other woman had successfully pulled his eye as this one has. Not since Lesego. He had forgotten how beautiful life could be. How pleasant love could feel.

"Hi Kamano," she said.

The lip gloss on her added a spark to her perfection.

"Doctor Komane." He pulled himself together to sit right.

"Please stop calling me that. It makes me uncomfortable," she complained.

"Ah, did you buy the title at Pick'n Pay?" he teased.

"Oh please." She rolled her eyes and lightly smiled. He began to drive. There was a shop at Mall of the North that she knew. They sold good suits at prices that didn't break the bank.

To their fortune, a perfect black fit was there for Kamano. It needed no adjustments.

"What?" Boikarabelo jumped up from the sofa, and some of the popcorn in her bowl got spilled.

"Khumo come and see your big brother here," she screamed.

Khumo pushed into the living room fast.

"Man," Khumo's eyes brightened. "Big brother you clean up good haa?"

"Of course," Kamano made a 360 degree turn to give his younger siblings a better look at him.

"You must learn from the best."

Kamano tapped Khumo's shoulder and passed to the kitchen for a glass of water. Their jaws were dropped. Kamano had not cared about how he looked since Lesego and the kids passed.

When he got to Safari River Estate, he stepped out of his red Polo noticing her. She looked like perfection. Her dress was completely black, with something that looked like a bow over the breast and over her shoulder. He had seen this woman dressed up many times but now, she was on another level. She smiled at him, and he wanted to melt in her unforgettable floral scent.

"You look like someone who plays for Barcelona," she complemented him, probably for the first time. His stomach tightened and he felt the strains of the previous day's training. It overwhelmed him that this beautiful brown-chocolate skinned woman saw him.

The wedding venue was a wonder of its own. It was at a lodge outside Polokwane and on the day, its prestige was elevated by themed decorations.

"Welcome to Katlego and Phil's wedding," someone at the entrance said. "Let me mark your names and show you where to go."

"Mmakoma Komane," Mmakoma said. The waiter browsed through and flipped to the next two pages. He was not finding her name on the list.

"Let's try Janet Komane." She nervously looked at Kamano who stood tall like being on that list meant nothing.

"Oh, Janet. Your seat is on table eleven. It's on the right."

Her parents were already seated. David Komane stood up to hug his daughter and he gave Kamano a handshake.

"Dad, this is my friend, Kamano," she said.

"Nice to meet you," David Komane said and sat down.

"Hi mom." She touched her mother's hand and sat next to her. Kamano took the seat after Mmakoma. He felt Alice Komane's eyes on him like a sharp piercing.

Mmakoma and her father started talking about something that was happening at Komane Civils. They got intensely engaged with it that Kamano hoped Mmakoma would not skip over her mother to sit next to her dad. It would leave no barrier between him and Alice who wasn't trying to be hospitable at all.

Alice started typing something on her phone. It seemed like a back and forth conversation.

There was a bit of noise at the back when four couples arrived together at once. Their number and familiarity with each other made it hard to not notice them.

"So typical of them," Alice disapproved their entourage.

"You know how Caiphas and his people are," David Komane made a joke, but Alice didn't laugh. The older couple of the four came to greet. The two older men seemed to know each other well. His wife followed behind him, then the rest of the family. Kamano figured that he probably should stand up for the handshakes.

"This is Kamano, Mmakoma's friend," David introduced Kamano to Caiphas.

"You must greet the young man with respect, he seems to be picking up the pieces well after your son's mess," David said to Caiphas jokingly.

The two timers laughed hard and passed. His sons and their wives followed in the pattern of their father and exchanged handshakes.

There was a strange exchange between Mmakoma and the couple that greeted them last. Unlike the others, she became reluctant to shake his hand. After his greeting, his wife behind him had a forced smile on and Mmakoma was equally discomfited.

"Who are they?" Kamano whispered to Mmakoma.

"They are the Makwela's."
She was brief.

"The last one to greet, is he your ex?"

"Yes, that's Lekau." She moved her face as if she was going to look at Kamano, but she avoided his eye.

"Oh," he sighed. "It makes sense."

"What makes sense Kamano?"

"You're tense around him. You still like him?" Kamano's forehead formed wrinkles.

"Naa, been over him for a while now," she reluctantly said. Could one fully be over a person with whom they had a child? She will probably always have a small room for Lekau in her heart.

"If you say so," Kamano sighed. On a normal day, the same words coming out of his mouth would have gone down as a joke. Not this time.

Alice's phone vibrated in her hand, the call made her edgy. Her thumb went in circles around the red button. Mmakoma stole a peek at the screen. She noticed a number with four sevens at the end. Alice eventually hit the red button and rejected the call. Then she asked to be excused and walked to the open area far from where people sat.

The call wasn't long but when she came back to her seat, the same number called again. She excused herself again. Mmakoma asked to be excused this time too. She passed behind her mother making her way to the bathroom.

"Do what I pay you to do Patrick. I can't leave this wedding to save the day. Handle it," Mmakoma overheard Alice as she passed behind her.

The bathroom was carved with limestone around the walls. Where limestone ended, wooden carvings began. Next to the door were large pots made from cement with pebbles stacked inside.

Mmakoma looked at her own reflection on the mirror and smiled at what she was about to get herself into. It was both exciting and frightening. She pulled her phone out of her clutch to check Patrick Zimba's phone number. It had four sevens at the end. It did. She couldn't help her own excitement.

She admired herself on the mirror one more time. Johnston Khaya had done an amazing job with the dress.

There was a flush from one of the toilets, then someone came out from one of the doors. It was Rebecca Makwela. The beautifully aging woman sparkled in a traditional Xhosa black and white dress. Her lips and nails were both painted red.

"Hi baby," she smiled. It dawned on Mmakoma how much she missed the woman's warmth.

Rebecca became like a mother to her from the moment she carried Mogau.

"Hi Mma," she said. Her heart glazed with joy.

"So nice to see you. You look amazing," Rebecca complemented her. She flushed tap water onto her palms and began to rub, letting the hand soap to foam and smoothly lather between her hands. She dried them and took out lotion from her bag.

"You look stunning yourself Mma."

"Thank you," Rebecca said, as she touched Mmakoma's back. They began to walk out of the bathroom.

"You have made yourself a stranger. You must visit sometimes."

"It would be nice to visit but imagine how Lekau's wife will feel finding me in your home," Mmakoma.

"You are overthinking this baby. You are practically family. She has to get used to that." Rebecca turned to look at Mmakoma who was behind her on the narrow pathway made out of stone.

"I will visit. I miss the family."

"We also miss you."

It was probably true that Rebecca missed her, but as for the entire family missing her, Mmakoma had her own doubts. The Makwela's watched each other's backs like hawks. The others kind of knew what was going on in her relationship with Lekau.

He might have never told them but when you are close to someone, you will pick up on these things, somehow.

Caiphas Makwela was the kind of man to protect his family with his life, even from matters of the heart sometimes. It was like him. In fact, it was like all the Makwela's, including Pogisho. You would swear she was born into the family and didn't come through marriage.

Kamano raised his head from his phone. Rebecca noticed him. He had a begrudged smile.

"Is that your new…" Rebecca was about to ask.

"No Mma, he's just my friend," Mmakoma cut in laughing.

"Okay." They held hands right to left and left to right. Whenever Rebecca would hold her that way, a hug or a forehead kiss followed.

"Lekau didn't tell me about his baby, you know Mma?" Mmakoma brought up her concern.

"His baby?" Rebecca.

"Yes, his son, Papi."

"No, Lekau has no son. They don't have a baby that I know of," Rebecca laughed, softly warding off the puzzle on her own face. "The only Papi I know belongs to Tumishang, Mmathapelo's sister."

"Oh," Mmakoma sighed. She was mortified. But she was also taken over by a whole new feeling. It was bizarre. When she was supposed to feel relief, another reality struck her hard. Her daughters now had family that she knew nothing about. She parked the thought somewhere in her and smiled at Rebecca who was now pulling to hug her.

"I'm going back to my seat."

Rebecca walked away from the warm embrace.

A song started playing and people got excited. Two children with white flowers walked in. When they got to the front, the music changed and an Afro pop song by Mafikizolo started to play. The groomsmen and bridesmaids danced their way to the front as everyone celebrated and older ladies began to ululate. The groom walked in with another song and waited in the front for his bride. There were no dance moves on his part, probably from nerves. There was much anticipated silence before the bride walked in. She looked like royalty in her white gown.

The matrimonial went on and there was a forty-five minutes break before the wedding reception commenced. Kamano and Mmakoma made their way to their assigned seats. Alice and David remained outside to mingle and talk to old friends.

Muzi came to their table with a popular actress. He greeted. Kamano said no word to him. He didn't nod nor smile.

"Is it necessary to stay for reception?" He spoke in a low tone as Muzi and his partner walked away.

"I don't think so," Mmakoma said.

"Let's go."

"Cool."

CHAPTER 11

The Komane Civils office in Polokwane lacked the appeal of the size of company it had grown into over the years. At least that's what Mmakoma thought. They were no longer just another BBBEE company that survived on crumbs and bribes. They were formidable within their space, it had to show. But David Komane loved simplicity. He was not one to release funds willy-nilly.

Mmakoma's black boots made a knocking sound as she got through the reception area. The new lady in a purple suit had a smile of familiarity. It was telling that she knew exactly who Mmakoma was. Mmakoma waved at her as she confirmed that

Khomotšo was already expecting her.

Her heeled boots continued to knock, more distinctively as she ascended the wooden staircases to make it to the HR manager's office.

She untied her grey trench coat feeling warmth from the air conditioner. Khomotšo pushed her chair backwards to relax and they began to converse. Mmakoma unveiled her eyes from the cover of her sunglasses, placing them on the table.

They'd spoken the night before that she would need some information from Khomotšo's database regarding some employees. She did not elucidate any further than that it was for survey purpose.

Khomotšo opened a file to let Mmakoma have a look. She offered Mmakoma a cup of coffee, but Mmakoma declined it. She wasn't planning to be there long enough to finish a whole cup. She wasn't one to drink coffee anyway. Khomotšo went downstairs to brew a cup for herself.

Mmakoma looked around before clicking into the file named Zimba. His contact details were there, along with details of his next-of-kin, work mileage, his house address, his bank account number, the whole thing.

Mmakoma raised her neck to listen for any steps that may be walking towards the office. She couldn't help her elation.

She quickly snapped the computer screen before closing Zimba's file. Then she printed a page with a list of their employees.

"I think this has everything I need," Mmakoma smiled at Khomotšo who was just coming in with her cup of coffee.

Although Komane Civils wasn't in her list of daily responsibilities, Mmakoma was always involved in decision-making. David wanted it that way.

She thanked Khomotšo and complemented her nails. Her shared love for the finer things in life exuded through her choice of clothing. That was the first thing that drew them to each other. It was a rare thing amongst all the other ladies who worked for Komane Civils. It was hard to discuss make-up, hair and style with any of them. She's had to settle for conversations about television shows and other things she didn't have profound interest in at company events.

She waved at the receptionist on her way out and jumped onto her car to make her way to the N1 site outside Polokwane.

The site was typical of any large-scale road construction site. A grader went up and down with some young fellows running back and forth by its side. The sun was out yet too weak to ward off the cold. It was freezing cold. But the lower temperatures must have been working in favour of the men who were jogging up and down to work the road, and maybe the women who held red flags to direct traffic.

"Thought I should pop in to see how things are on this site," she said to Luwellan, the site manager who was standing in his white container office.

His body was ballooned by the thick and bright orange safety jacket with reflecting strips around the chest area and arms.

"You came on a good day. We have a walk-about in thirty minutes. It would be great if you join us," he said.

"I'd love to, but I have a meeting in an hour's time," she said helping herself to a seat. She hadn't brought safety boots with her. It was a weird thing, almost unacceptable to be anywhere in a construction site with high heels.

"The site looks good. How's the team? How's Patrick?"

"The team is doing great. They are really going out of their way to make this site a success. Patrick also, he's really been pushing them. I'm proud," Luwellan.

"Good to know," Mmakoma nodded, and her ponytail wiggled. She still had her sunglasses on. Luwellan also had his.

"Where is he now, on site?" Mmakoma.

"You mean Patrick? He's on site. Let me give him a call."

"No, I was just asking. Don't call," she giggled sheepishly.

"It's a crazy day for him," Luwellan said passively.

"I told him that he must leave the site running smoothly while he's on leave."

"He's going on leave?"

"From tomorrow till next Wednesday. It's a well-deserved break."

She remembered that some leave-days could be arranged on sites and only be updated into the system later.

She left the site for a part of Polokwane that she had never been to before. The houses were old in style, typically three-bedrooms. There was nothing particularly off about the area. It was a slow and quiet part of town, probably a good area to raise a family.

The address on her notes led to the third house on the stretched street. She drove slowly past the face-brick house with an old-style Tuscan roof. There were no cars outside nor any giveaway to confirm that it was indeed his house.

The area suited a man like Patrick Zimba though. He was a family man who loved his wife and children. It was like him to use every opportunity to mention either one of them in a conversation. Anyone who knew him knew this about him. He and his wife came from Zambia but have been in South Africa for so long that you would easily forget the fact.

His command of Sepedi was above average. As for speaking IsiZulu, it was like he was born speaking the language. He had the accent right, you would miss him for someone from KZN. It now made sense because the man listed IsiNgoni as his home language. It must be a lot like IsiZulu. Mmakoma bent her lips downwards to agree with her own thoughts.

She reached the end of the long street and wondered if coming to that side of town was worth her while. She decided to make a U-turn to pass the house one last time before going home. At this point she was beginning to laugh at her ambition and why it had excited her. But it was silly.

A black Range Rover entered the driveway of the house she was eyeing. She couldn't see the number plate, but it was the same kind as her mother's. Another car was behind it. A grey double cab. Her palms began to sweat as her eyes popped. What were the odds?

To her left was a street forming a T-junction with the one she was on. She took it without hesitation, lest she be noticed. Something sinister was happening. Now she was sure of it.

She hit a hump and swore between her teeth. It didn't help her to calm down. Her mind was racing. All the way her apartment. Her curiosity demanded satisfaction now. It demanded attention and she could no longer put it at bay. She tossed and turned between her sheets trying to calm herself and to ignore the different scenarios her mind couldn't help but make up.

Kamano was in black tracksuits, feet on the coffee table and remote in his hand.

"Come in," he said carelessly, hearing a knock.

"Doc." He pulled his feet off the table. Gasping, he immediately sat upright.

"Glad I found you." She sat on the sofa next to him.

"Can I please borrow your car for a few days." She sounded erratic, something different from her typical composure.

"Why?" Kamano pulled his face up.

"My car has been giving me problems and I am not in the space to get it checked right now. I know it's a stretch to ask but I need someone who knows cars better to drive it for a few days and let me know."

Kamano placed his hand over his mouth wanting to laugh. Women expected men to just know what to do with broken cars. Nonetheless, it was better him stranded than her.

"It's fine," he agreed.

"Thank you so much," she leaned and hugged him. He pulled a heroic macho smile. Her scent registered in his mind. It was something he had never smelt before, feminine yet classy, as she was.

Kamano took her outside to explain some of his

car's faults and flaws that she would need to know before driving. It wasn't like her Mercedes Benz. Some things needed to be explained.

"I hope you are not planning to perform crimes with my car."

"Not at all. It has a tracker, doesn't it?"

"It does, but you sound really shady right now," he bantered.

"Please Kamano. I will take care of it well. I mean, look at my Benz. Extraordinary."

"And mine is just ordinary?"

"Isn't it?" she laughed, he also laughed.

"Here," he handed her the keys

"Thanks, it will be back without a scratch."

"I hope so."

She parked the Polo at the shops a few houses away from Zimba's house. There was a medical journal on the rear seat. She began to read it, passing time.

Two hours passed without a sign of activity from Patrick Zimba's house. Nature was also calling. She pulled the handle on the door of the Polo to get out. Placing her feet on the ground, she noticed a grey double cab enter the parking lot with speed. It was the same one he saw Patrick Zimba driving when he was leaving her mother's house.

She pressed herself back into the Polo and moved her eyes around for something to cover herself with.

Kamano had a navy-blue bucket hat labelled with the Department of Education's logo on the back seat. She reached for it. She covered her head with it and waited for Zimba to come out of the store.

She giggled within her stomach. The blend of fear and excitement was pleasant.

Her phone vibrated. Kamano's name was on screen.

"Doc, how's it there? Is the car still fine?" he said.

"Yeah. I should be asking you,"

"I'm the coolest principal today. You should have seen these boys flood around me this morning. They think I bought a new car," he laughed.

"Can I call you back," she switched. Patrick Zimba was coming out of the store, three grocery bags in his hands.

He was barely inside his yard when his wife came out. He gave her one bag and hugged her. Then he got into the car and reversed.

"Kamano, I have to attend to something quickly. Can I call you back?" she repeated before hanging up.

She trailed behind the double cab, keeping a distance. They drove outside town, passing past vast farming land with green hills. It was in the direction of Magoebaskloof. Several farms with tall trees of timber shadowed over the road and gave her a feeling of being small in a big world. Her heart began to pump hard as she came across fewer and fewer cars. She laughed as a check to her own sanity. She allowed cars in between them and hoped that her distance was enough not to raise suspicion.

Patrick took a turn into a small gravel road that had a small gate ahead. Mmakoma drove past.

About half a kilometre from the gravel road, she made a U-turn. She parked the car on the side, before the road curvature. Thatches outside the timber farm were tall enough to conceal the car for the most part.

There was her promise to return the car without a scratch. She pulled her face at the sound of a screech. She also crossed her fingers for the tyres as she hid her purse under the seat.

It was getting real. It was exciting. The blend of fear and anticipation together roused in her. She could stop and pray first, but it was one of those moments that she just didn't want to hear God. But she still wanted to be back in one piece and alive.

"Father, just keep me safe, please." Like that, her prayer was done. She had ticked her box.

She pressed the key one more time. The car was locked. She was stealthy between the thatches and eventually she went over the fence. The timber trees were magnificently tall, she felt like an ant moving in between them line by line.

She stopped where the trees ended. Ahead was an open veld after the remains of chopped trees. Numerous tree stumps still attached to the ground.

There was an old building about half a kilometre from where she was. It looked like an old workshop. The grey double cab was parked outside.

Mmakoma covered her mouth as she maintained her crouched position. Her wig started to feel itchy around her neck. She took it off, put it on the ground, and wore the bucket hat again. It helped that she was in loafers and not the high heels of the day before.

Patrick came out of the building. He looked around then got into his car and drove out.

Mmakoma froze in silent fear as the car got closer, then passed.

"God, this is it," she whispered to herself as she sprung out of the woods. She'd heard many stories of farmers shooting unsuspecting trespassers from far range and it made her fear even more. But she had to get to the building and see why a man like Zimba would take leave to visit such a place.

The area around the workshop was well kept. The grass was cut and there was a clear area all around.

Mmakoma peeped into a hole on the corrugated iron. She pushed the door, but it did not open. It was locked. She climbed onto the stacked bricks at the back to catch a glimpse through the window. Her foot slipped and she hit the corrugated iron. It banged, sending a shiver up her spine.

But there was a sound reaching her ears now. A murmuring of some sort. She scanned the room.

Her hair was leaving the scalp. It felt like it. She jumped down.

The murmuring got louder. Much louder. Hard to ignore. Frightening.

She moved to the next window. It was high. She looked around for something to climb. She went for the bricks. She stacked a few together and she could rise and see.

Slipping and almost falling off, she clasped her hand tighter on the frame. There was a woman tied to a pole. She was on a mattress. That was as much as she could see through the dusty window. Shivers went through her entire body.

I should call the police.

She breathlessly sped to other sides of the building to find a way in. Her phone wasn't with her. She touched her hips searching and realised that she'd left it in the car.

She had to push the door again and again. It was really locked.

She went around one more time. One of the windows was lower than others. Just a little. She unstacked some bricks from the stack and began to tower them before that window.

If Mr Zimba comes back and finds me here. I'm dead.

For the first time in the many years she had known Patrick Zimba, he was a fearsome man. His very dark skin felt like a cover for some sort of deep darkness inside. She was afraid.

She elevated her body holding dearly to a part of the corrugated iron. With a brick, she broke the glass. The brittle material broke into pieces and shattered when it hit the ground. One pierced her skin with impact. Her blood was already boiling, nullifying the pain of the moment.

She was frantic. She had to get to the woman. She raised her leg and felt the fabric of her trousers tear.

She was able to hop in. She hit her hands against each other, but no dust flew off. The dirt was stuck on her, mixed with the sweat of her palms.

There was an opening ahead. The frames no longer had a door. Old brown and cream steel office furniture haphazardly floated all over the room.

Her breath began to pace with the drumming of her heart. The middle section of the building was spacious. And empty. It felt like no man's land. Exposed. A place where a bullet could be sent from far and not miss you.

The woman was on the other end. There was a door to that end. Mmakoma ran to the other side pushed the door open. It wasn't locked.

"Janet," the woman murmured her name through the mouth covering. Her eyes were circled in darkness.

"Naledi?" Mmakoma said as she touched her all over. It was hard to decide where to begin.

"How does your baby feel?" she asked her,

pulling her mouth cover down. She touched her shoulders to give her shaking body comfort. She twitched as Mmakoma tried to touch her bump. It had grown bigger since.

The sound of car tyres rolling through gravel was approaching. The two ladies gazed into each other's eyes. The tyres were getting closer and closer.

"Go to the other side. They won't see you there," Naledi said. Mmakoma shook her head.

"Hide," Naledi reiterated firmly. Desperately. Mmakoma touched her face and covered her mouth. She sprinted past the large middle room, to the side that had furniture lying all over. She found an old office cabinet full of dust to hide behind, then she covered her nose with her blouse and hoped that her sinuses wouldn't react.

Someone opened a car door. Then another. Then two doors were shut. There was a difference in how they sounded. It was two cars outside.

Two people inaudibly exchanged words and one began to unlock the door.

Mmakoma felt a sneeze coming and held it back with all her might. She stood up to get a bit of air from the broken window. She reverted to her ready-to-hop position and froze again.

"Little girl." It was Alice's voice.

Mmakoma's eyes popped.

"You are stubborn. Too stubborn for your own good," Dr Alice Komane.

"Patrick, give her some water. I need her thinking straight."

There was a shrivelling sound, like something was being taken out of a plastic.

"There's a scent in here." Alice sniffed. "There's a smell of perfume."

Mmakoma girded herself in a squatted position. Her occasional squats came in handy. She was ready to fight or flee.

Her mother called out the perfume's name. It was the one she had bought for her in London.

"Look around Patrick. There's definitely someone in here. This is a limited-edition scent."

Mmakoma could hear Patrick's footsteps. Her eyes began to measure what it would take to go up the window and take flight. Her better mind argued that it was her own mother on the other side. Courage suddenly arose out of her fear.

"Mr Zimba." She walked out of her hiding place. Patrick moved closer with the shrewdest face of him she'd ever seen. Cold and unrelenting. He wasn't the same man who smiled and joked and spoke non-stop.

He held her arm tight and pushed her forward.

"No need for that. I'm not trying to run," Mmakoma said turning her face towards the strong man with very dark skin and greying moustache. He wasn't the same. He was like a stranger to her.

"I knew it was you. Very few people have that

perfume," Alice said.

"Mom, how could you?"

"Keep your two cents to yourself Janet. You know nothing."

Alice gave her daughter that disciplinary look that always got her to straighten up and behave. Mmakoma struggled with the look. It took her back to the time when she was a little girl. She wrestled with the feeling of being that little girl who was taught to straighten up and look befitting. That girl who desired her mother but could never find her, no matter how close she was.

"What now? Are you going to kill us both?" she rebelled.

"Tie her up Patrick," Alice said.

"Mom, this is wrong," Mmakoma cried out. "You are evil."

"You and I are the same. We are cut from the same cloth," Alice Komane moved her head sideways to show Patrick where he must sit her daughter.

"I'm not like you. I would never do such evil." Mmakoma wrenched her hand as Patrick tied her.

"Oh please. Where is Dipuo's sister? Or brother? You don't even know what that baby would have been," Alice said piously. Mmakoma's eyeballs widened.

"Hm, you thought I didn't know that?" Alice's eyebrows curved, as a knowing smile took over her bright, minimally aging face.

"You are just like me. We do what we have to do."

Mmakoma's eyes twinkled. She desired to erase the exposure and the disconcerting feeling that came over her. That of a perturbation that never ever left her mind. Sometimes she succeeded at suppressing it far into the subconscious, but never permanently. Would it have been a son? Or would it have been a daughter? Would she have loved ice-cream and dolls, or maybe sports and cars?

Alice pulled an orange crate that had served as a tray to carry twelve bottles of cool drink at some point. The bottles themselves were nowhere near sight. She sat on the crate. Her feet inside red track pants and a matching track top were comfortably placed apart. The hierarchy of the room was set. It was clear. Alice Komane was right there on top.

"How did you get here?" she asked as she watched her daughter being harnessed and attached to the pole like Naledi was.

Mmakoma looked at her mother from the corner of her eyes. Her blood was beginning to boil. She made a light sigh that she tried to conceal.

"Where did you park your car?" Alice spoke more sharply. Her tone demanded an answer.

"I didn't come with it." Mmakoma dropped her eyes. "I took a taxi."

"There are no taxis coming here," Alice.

"Unless you're willing to pay." Mmakoma.

Alice's eyes moved from her daughter to her phone screen.

Patrick Zimba standing by the side with a woollen brown jersey that had diamond patterns in front. The man never brought his face in Mmakoma's direction.

"Janet, you and I know what it means to let go of something precious," Alice Komane said.

Naledi moved in discomfort on her mattress. Patrick Zimba looked at Alice. Then he walked out.

"I hope you'll be talking sense into your friend because if she does not make the right choice, I am going to multiply pain in her life," Alice said.

"You'd have to kill me first before you get away with it," Mmakoma said boldly. Alice was amused.

The corrugated iron door banged, and Zimba walked back in. He had a paper container in his hand and a plastic on his other. He cut the container in two and distributed the food.

CHAPTER 12

Kamano began to fidget, moving back and forth and around his office table. She hadn't returned his calls. Five of them.

He picked up his house keys that had the Polo spare keys on them. He also grabbed Mmakoma's car keys and locked his office. Mmakoma sounded fine last time they spoke. But something was just off. He couldn't shake it off.

Mrs Mabitsela's eyes were glued to the computer screen when he passed the reception area. He stopped by her window and told the full figured fifty-something year old woman that he was off.

"Are you okay?" Her face expressed concern.

She looked at her watch. It was still 13h00 and Kamano usually left the school around 15h30 on days when he had soccer practice and 16h00 every other day. Leaving before everyone else was an anomaly for him.

"I'm okay. See you tomorrow."

He didn't stop to feed her unsaid order for an explanation. She had a way to politely demand explanations without saying a word. He hated it sometimes.

He briskly walked into the hospital, almost passing Boikarabelo chatting to someone at reception.

"Big brother."

She was happy.

"Hi Boi." He waved and walked past. She ran behind him.

"You are acting weird. Why are you here? Why are you running?" she interrogated in a manner that teased him.

"None of your business. Get off me, I'm in the middle of something right now," Kamano said.

"You're in the middle of Dr J."

She laughed at her brother. "It's her car you've been cruising in. I knew you liked her."

"Boi, I'll see you at home. I need to see Doc right away."

He was rushing through the long hallway. She was

breathlessly jogging behind him.

"Everything okay doctor?" a porter asked.

"Everything's good," she replied, and slowed down. Then she laughed and turned back.

"I'm sorry Sir but I can't get hold of Dr Komane for a better explanation. Please understand." Charlene's cheeks were flushed in frustration as she explained to a tall man with a toddler in his arms.

Kamano was surprised by the number of people that filled the waiting area. He had never found so many at a time. None of them bore a welcoming face.

"Just like all the other doctors. No respect for other people's time." The man spewed frustration and others agreed from their seats.

"Good afternoon Sir," Kamano intervened, the man nodded back in acknowledgment.

"Charlene, how are you?"

"I'll be better if I could find Dr Komane." she motioned her head from left to right, her eyes twinkling in distress. There was an undeniable expectation in her tone.

Kamano feared for the worst. He felt distress rise. He felt fear find him again. He couldn't lose again. He feared the man he would become if he lost one more time.

He equally reciprocated Charlene's expectation

for answers, "Have you tried every possible way to find her."

"Yes? I've even tried her mom and her house, nothing," she explained.

He rubbed his hands against each other and fixed his belt. He turned around to face the expectant faces in the room.

"Good afternoon, everyone," he addressed the aggravated patients.

"I know that some of you have been here for quite some time. Thank you for your patience. I am not here to replace the doctor, but to explain to all of you that there are some unforeseen issues that have come up and the doctor is unable to make it here today. May you please forgive us. None of us expected it. I will ask you to please go home. Charlene will contact all of you to reschedule."

"She could have informed us hours ago and not make us sit here waiting for the doctor who's never coming." One woman complained from the brown sofa.

"She was also unaware. I apologise on her behalf," Kamano said.

"Aargh, I should have booked Dr Flanagan. Our people are never professional." Another woman said leaving.

"Thank you all so much for understanding," Kamano said as the number of people began to dwindle.

"Thank you so much," Charlene murmured.

"They were so angry, and I didn't know what to do anymore."

"Maybe we should call the police," Kamano said.

"Isn't it best that we let her mom do it?"

"You're right," Kamano sighed unsatisfactorily.

"The police require twenty-four hours or forty-eight hours before reporting a missing person," Charlene reasoned.

The wrinkle that formed on her cheek gave away a lack of toleration for how the system worked. She wasn't a fan of how the government was running the country.

"I suppose," Kamano said in a disengaged tone. All his attention was on his phone.

"I'll print out a note to explain that we are closed," Charlene said.

"Yeah, do that," Kamano took a red pen from his chest pocket.

"Here's my number. Please message me yours. Let me know if you hear anything."

He dashed out of the practice in a blaze. His car was parked somewhere on the roadside according to his tracking app. He tried to silence the thoughts as he drove there. He inhaled deep and exhaled softly to calm the storm that was brewing within. He had no room to nurse those feelings. He had to shut every temptation to entertain his worst fears. But the car had been stationary for hours. That was a fact.

"Khums," he said to his brother on the phone. "Where are you?"

"I'm home. What's happening?"

"I might miss Sally-Anne's play tonight."

"It's okay, I'm here, she will be fine. What's going on with you?"

"Something's not right with Doc. I'm on my way to check."

"Sure. Let me know how it goes," Khumo said.

"Sure," Kamano.

His heart paced harder as he neared the location of the car. The road hardly had any traffic. It curved just after a gravel road leading into a farm. There were tall trees on both sides. He was in a 4Matic, but it felt sandwiched by the tall trees on both sides. The scenery was breath-taking, but he had no iota of appreciation left in him. Too much was at stake.

As he curved with the road, there was his VW Polo. It looked deserted. He parked behind, touched the door and cautiously paused.

"God not again, please." He closed his eyes.

He pushed the door open and started looking around the Polo. He pressed his spare key and it flickered.

Mmakoma's handbag was under the seat. It wasn't like her to go without her bag. Criminals wouldn't leave it behind either. The bag was a commodity worth a few monthly salaries of an ordinary man.

He tossed it in the boot and looked at the newly

formed path. Thatch lied down the narrow pathway leading into the farm of tall trees.

He followed the path and skipped over to the other side of the fence. The ground beneath the trees had neither grass nor thatch. The shoe prints on it were clear. He trailed them until he noticed a wig on the ground. He felt rage and inspiration to go further. He looked around. His eyes picked up a building. Two cars were parked outside.

This is my location- he typed a text to Khumo.

There was no signal under the tall trees, but he hoped that somehow, once he made it out of the woods, the message would go through.

One car, the SUV was revved out. Carefully he watched it. The sight of a familiar face in the car brought him immense relief. He wanted to run up to Dr Alice Komane, to wave at her. At that point he cared too little for the lack of welcome he had sensed from her when they met at the wedding. Mmakoma's life could have been at stake and their care for her was something they had in common.

He stayed hidden and watched instead. His message was still there. It hadn't gone through.

He tried to phone Khumo but the call wasn't going through. Khumo was eight years his junior, but he was in the military. He'd know what such circumstances meant and what to do.

The second car, the double cab drove out ten minutes later. The driver was a man of a dark hue of brown in his fifties.

Not, Alice Komane? An affair? He chuckled. Then he shook his head. Mmakoma must be spying on her mother. But where was she?

He sprinted out of the woods towards the building as the sound of the grey double cab disappeared.

He pushed the door. It was locked, so he went around the building. There was a broken window. He peeped in and noticed the disorganised, dusty furniture. Eeuw, Couldn't they find a better place?

His phone vibrated in his pocket. His message had gone through and Khumo's reply was prompt.

Thanks. I'm on my way.- Khumo

I'm fine. Who owns this place?- Kamano

I'll let you know- Khumo.

There was a humming sound from inside. It was the sound of someone trying to scream but couldn't. Kamano slowly moved towards the broken window. He peeped in. There was no sign of people. But the humming persisted. He decided to jump in and carefully went around the old furniture, trying to make as little of a sound as possible. He looked into the emptiness of the hall. Then he looked at the door on the other side. The murmuring came from there. He went for it. He pushed the door. It made a screeching sound, but opened.

His heart smiled as he saw Mmakoma smile with

her beautiful eyes behind the mouth covering. The other woman was lying down on the mattress.

He untied her mouth and embraced her. He looked around for something to cut the harness with, but there was nothing. He kissed her forehead and felt himself release tension. And fear. She was alive. He could still do something about it.

His eyes searched for a sharp object. There was nothing around. He walked to the room that had office furniture and searched. Nothing was sharp enough.

He remembered the pair of scissors he'd left at the back of his Polo and hoped that Mmakoma hadn't removed it. He climbed out of the window and sprinted for the Polo. If there was a moment he was grateful for waking up to run on some mornings, that was it.

The gate was a simple farm gate with a chain, but it wasn't locked. His wheels lifted the dust from the farm road as anxiety rose within him. He shouldn't have left them alone like that. The car was too slow. It felt like decades to get back into the workshop. When he did, he cut loose the harnesses on both women and they both helped the pregnant woman up. She struggled to climb the furniture and to make it out of the window. Mmakoma went first to be able to help her from the outer end.

"You can drive your car. I'll drive mine behind

you."

In a motion of the head, she disagreed. He didn't argue. They left.

His arm were stretched out to the steering wheel and his face lacking expression. He made no effort for conversation.

The old grey shirt he had on was torn, and dust was all over him.

She looked at him and felt undeserving. His perfectly ironed chinos were not spared from the dirt. It contrasted the perfect lines that divided the middle of both his legs. The lines had been ironed and perfected so many times that they were now white, paralleling all the way down his thighs and eventually to his shoes.

"I didn't want them to spot me in that car. They know it." She was apologetic.

"Is that why you borrowed my car?"

His eyes remained on the road ahead. He was a bruised a little by her dishonesty.

"I will call for it to be towed." She didn't answer his question. He kept driving. When he checked his mirrors, he realised that the pregnant woman had fallen asleep.

CHAPTER 13

Kamano had been quiet the whole way and now he was taking them into a house in Seshego. He didn't ask, he didn't explain. He just took them there.

Mmakoma made several attempts to converse with him on the way, but it was to no avail. He was acerbic and disengaged. His answers were flat.

It was strange that she was more in comfort with that version of Kamano than the one she had witnessed of a woman she knew all her life.

"We are here." He pulled the hand brake and pushed the door of the car open.

"What are we doing here?" Mmakoma ran her eyes around the peach house with paving all around except at the back where the soil was hard. It looked like it was once a vegetable garden.

"We should be safe here, until I figure out what to do next," he said.

Naledi yawned from the back. She opened the door and pushed her belly out before her body. She followed Kamano's lead without question.

The house was clean inside, but it had the aura of emptiness, not from the lack of furniture, but from the lack of occupation. There was a large photo with three children on the wall. One was a baby and the eldest one was shy of ten years of age.

"Please settle in. We'll figure out what to do next from here," Kamano repeated as he flushed out tap water from the sink.

On the opposing wall was a family portrait with the same three children, two standing and one held by Kamano next to a woman with a tender smile. They looked like a happy family. Next to it was a painting. The painting was that of Kamano and the beautiful woman smiling into each other's eyes. They looked very much in love.

"Is this your house?" Mmakoma asked.

"Yes," Kamano quickly moved his eyes away from her. He rinsed the glass in his hand and poured some water. He inspected the colour of the water. It was clear.

"Have some," he offered Naledi a glass.

"Thank you," she said.

"Call your kids and Charlene and let them know that you are fine. Maybe call towing services too."

He handed his phone to her.

"I'm going to the shops for food and essentials. Is there anything specific you will need?"

"I can do with soap and lotion," Mmakoma said. Kamano stuck his thumb in the air and left after Naledi confirmed that she was fine. Mmakoma walked from room to room exploring the house. The memorabilia of the woman who once lived in the house was at every turn, untouched. Mmakoma touched her dear heart at the realisation of her envy. Kamano must have loved the woman with all his breath to have kept her presence intact in her absence. She desired to be loved like that. Her eyes filled as she searched her entire life for evidence of anyone who'd cared about her as much. She couldn't find any.

She pulled some air in to press tears back, and strolled back to where Naledi was silent and seated.

"What are we going to do now?" she asked her.

"I want to go back home," Naledi said.

"Isn't that too obvious. They will easily find you. Who knows what they will do to you?"

"If they wanted to do anything to me, they would have done it by now." Naledi pursed her lips.

"Are you not afraid for your life?" Mmakoma.

"Your mother is evil, to the core, but she's not a killer."

"I've dealt with people more cruel than her." Naledi showed no fear, her bulging belly was more prominent than ever.

"What will you do if they find you?"

"Demand my worth," Naledi said. "All your mother wants is for me not to embarrass her by making my pregnancy public. She wants me to go on as if I never had a baby by David Komane. She doesn't want me dead."

There was a pause before she continued talking. Mmakoma felt frustrated by the mention of her father's name.

"I want money. She wants me out of her face. She had better pay up, then both of us win."

"Wow," Mmakoma lifted her eyebrows, and rubbed the one on her right with her hand.

"You say you've dealt with people crueller than her?"

"My first born. He's the son of a Zimbabwean billionaire. That man's wife is on another level of cruel. But she ended up paying me." She wore a smile of victory.

"So, you are sorted with money?" Mmakoma.

"I've run out. My life is expensive."

"And what will happen when you're out again?"

"I'm a woman of my word. I never return to haunt anyone," Naledi said, leading the silence that followed.

The gate opened and Kamano drove in.

Mmakoma's heart began to throb. She was no longer at ease.

He placed the plastic on the dining area table and headed for the bathroom without a word to them. Naledi was falling asleep again on the sofa. Kamano brought a blanket.

"You can sleep anywhere in the house," he said walking away to enter the main bedroom.

There was soon a sound of water showers. Mmakoma reclined on the other sofa and fell asleep there.

CHAPTER 14

There was a smooth breeze that tenderly brushed over Kamano's skin, making the sharp rays of the morning sun somewhat forgivable. The mobile phone on his ear was interfering with the thoughts that were forming like a cloud in his mind. He walked further into what used to be a green and colourful vegetable garden. He remembered it at its prime, with green peppers and red peppers glazing in between the greenery. Now the soil was hardened, exposing years of not being tilled and turned.

A vague flashback of Lesego picking up some spinach hit his mind fleetingly. He embraced the memory like he had begun to do a few months ago.

"Principal Kgopa..." Mrs Mabitsela answered the

phone on the other end. He made a joke about calling her on her mobile phone instead of the school line. Like always, the near-retirement aged woman laughed gracefully. She had always joked that had she been much younger, she would have made sure that a man like Kamano never stayed single for too long. As much as that was a light joke, it had a way of opening up light conversations that helped him to absorb different facets of his pain and loss.

"I called to let you know that everything is on you today. I ain't comin."

"Today will be the school's best day ever," she replied.

As an experienced administrator, she knew the workings of the school like the palm of her own hand. Kamano could rely on her. Rosina Diale was a capable vice principal, but she has never been one to care about the personal issues of their learners. This made her rigid in her approach and leadership. This was a trait he appreciated but also felt blessed to have Mrs Mabitsela. She was the heart of the school.

Mmakoma came and sat on the window seal next to him. He concluded the conversation and placed his phone in his pocket. Mmakoma's gaze at his bare feet was unrelenting and unapologetic. He knew what she wanted to say, but she said nothing. She was unusually timid. It was subtle, but to Kamano it was as clear as day.

It was a bit shameful how robust and acidic he

became the day before. The thought made him want to bury his head in the sand. But he wasn't going to apologise for it. He could have lost her.

"Good morning," she said. He could tell from how her voice sounded that those were her first two words for the day.

"Good morning," he smiled. It came naturally to smile at every first glance of Mmakoma.

"Thanks for the toothbrush. That was very thoughtful of you."

"That was more for me. Imagine having to deal with your bad breath on such a beautiful morning. No way," he plagued her. She rolled her eyes within a soft smile, making his face tingle. He rubbed his cheeks down to keep himself in check.

A momentary sense of guilt struck him. It was eating at him that the first time he returned to the home he and Lesego shared was now, with a woman. Not just any other woman, but the one he wants and desires. He brushed the thought away.

"How did you sleep?" he asked.

"I slept well," she squinted her eyes as they received the bright morning rays of the Limpopo sun. They were dark and brown, so was her smooth chocolate skin.

The sun was blazing but the cold breeze was a comforting reminder that winter had arrived.

"How is she?" he asked.

"Better than I imagined she would be,"

Mmakoma said. "She asked to be taken home."

"Why?"

"It looks like she wants to be found," Mmakoma giggled nervously. Kamano's face turned towards her in disbelief.

"Doc, what's going on here?" he asked. Mmakoma made a miming sound as if she was trying to get her thoughts in place.

"I don't even know where to begin."

"Why would she want to be found?" Kamano. Mmakoma breathed in and out and gazed at him. The sun hit her smooth brown skin just right, the melanin was popping, perfect before his eyes.

"It's unbelievable, I know. But she insists," Mmakoma said. A screeching sound came from the door. Something that Kamano noticed the night before and made a mental note to oil the pivots.

A protruding bump led Naledi as she came out of the house. She greeted them before asking Kamano to take her home. His eyes immediately went to Mmakoma but in silence she made him know that it was best to just take her home.

"Don't forget to get yourself checked when you get home." Mmakoma broke the eye connection.

"But you've checked me, I'm fine. It's not like something happened," Naledi.

"Just do it Naledi. I did it without equipment. Do it to be sure."

Kamano went to freshen up. The ladies were

already ready. They drove to Ga- Ramongoana, a village not too far from Seshego. He knew how to get there because of a soccer game the Polokwane Rovers once had there. But it also wasn't too far from Ga-Semenya where he once taught.

Naledi pointed a house. There was an old man sitting outside with his walking stick resting against the white old-style garden chair made from wires that were crossed against each other to form squares. The house door was open and at the stopping of the car engine, a young woman came out of the house with a baby on her shoulder.

"That's my sister," Naledi said as she opened the door to come out. Mmakoma had taken Kamano's car doors off child lock while she had it.

The old man stood up from his chair to follow the young woman with a baby.

"Naledi," the sister's joy was undeniable. "We were so worried about you."

"I'm here now," Naledi said, embracing her sister in a tight hug. It could have been tighter had it not been for her baby bump. She introduced both Kamano and Mmakoma to his sister and grandfather, referring to them as her friends.

Kamano's phone rang. He looked at it and apologised to the old man and the ladies with a facial expression.

"Buti KK, are you okay? Khumo says that you've been at your house." It was a phone call from

Boikarabelo.

"I'm okay nana," he said.

"I hope so." She wasn't convinced.

"Is that Dr Komane in the background?" Mmakoma was laughing at something the old man said to her.

"Yes," Kamano said.

"I was going to call her after this call because she also hasn't been to work in... wait, wait. You're with her?" Boikarabelo.

"Ncaa, I thought you were calling for something serious."

He hung up.

The drive on R521 back to Seshego turned into uncomfortable silence for a while.

"Doc, why did you lie?" Kamano broke into the thick of it.

"Haa," Mmakoma murmured.

"I can't pretend to understand what's going on here, but more than that, you lied," he said.

"I couldn't share with anyone until I knew exactly what was going on."

"I have a problem with that."

He kept his face on the road, his eyes squinting dryly.

"It's not that deep Kamano. Come on," she giggled.

"I can't protect you when you lie to me."

He pulled his lip back, forming a dimple-like

wrinkle.

"It's not like my mother was going to kill me," she nervously giggled.

"I can't lose you Doc."

"It's not like you have me," she said casually.

He went into another sprout of silence before asking her where she wanted to go.

"We can pick up my and purse from your house and then you take me to my house. My daughters must be asking questions by now," she said.

"Cool," he said before tapping into quietness again.

He came back to an empty and quiet house after taking Mmakoma to Flora Park. The sound of keys dropping on the dining table made him think of it. He looked at the family portrait before his eyes and remembered the day like it was yesterday. His team had just won a soccer game and he was tired but Lesego insisted on a family photo shoot. She would have been upset if he postponed it again. He tiredly drove to the studio after his game, making it ten minutes late. She wasn't happy about it but the joy of him arriving became greater.

Little did he know that all the family photos, all the family outings and camps were for him. All of them. He put his palm over his heart. If only he knew that all those memories would be for him to cherish alone after they were all gone. The dreams and plans for their future were wiped out before him, with them. His desire to see his children and their children was wasted. Gone and lost forever. He was a man without a lineage. His knees got weak. He sat down.

For everywhere his eyes rested, he had a memory of Lesego. But that image was fading. He closed his eyes to bring it back, but his mind wasn't grasping it. He felt guilty. Guilty that he was forgetting his wife, and his precious children.

The conversation he had with Mrs Mabitsela the week before came to his mind. Her husband had passed on fifteen years ago, but she was still not used to the emptiness of her bed. She said it had gotten better with the years, but she still remembered him.

"I had to find my way without him," she had explained. Kamano remembered the black pen that was in her hand. She had stopped writing to tell him about missing her husband that morning. She did that from time to time, especially since Kamano's loss of Lesego and the kids.

"Do you think you found it? I mean a way to go on without Him?" Kamano had asked her that morning.

"I have," she had said.

"It took me years because I felt guilty every time I

experienced some sort of happiness. That held me back for a long time."

Kamano wondered if he was hinged in that cycle still. After going back into the soccer field and finding form again, he thought that he was over everything.

But being back in his house cut him deep. He walked into the main bedroom once again. The place used to be a haven when Lesego was still alive. Their wedding photo was still by their bedside.

He had entertained another woman. He wasn't proud of it. He wanted to kneel and pray but there were no words to begin the conversation with God. Nothing. He sang.

CHAPTER 15

"Are you at your house?" Alice said to Mmakoma on the phone.

"You're not planning to kidnap me, right?" Mmakoma.

"Come on," Alice.

"You can come, we need to talk anyway," Mmakoma said. Her mother was there within an hour. Dipuo ran to the door and embraced her. You could rely on her care-free personality to break barriers and dig deep for love and affection. Jumping to embrace her mother was something Mmakoma had never done in her childhood and even now in adulthood, her mother still didn't issue out hugs willy-nilly. With exception for Dipuo of course.

"I wanted to stay and tell you about my piano lessons, but mom says we must go with Aunty Khabo." The child told her grandmother.

"You must listen to your mother," Alice patted the child's back and opened her arms for Mogau who wasn't saying much. Khabonina was already at the door waiting for the girls.

"Your father is flying back tonight, and he wants us to have dinner tomorrow."

"Oh," Mmakoma said, gazing at her mother's face.

"You're not going to make it awkward," Alice said instructively.

Something in her tone made it clear that she wasn't expecting any objection.

"Of course." Mmakoma maintained her gaze.

"Good."

She picked her bag and placed her mobile phone inside and startled at her daughter's face.

"You're not going to ask anything?" she said.

"You're not going to say anything?" Mmakoma replied.

"Don't take up that tone with me. I'm still your mother," Alice.

"Of course," Mmakoma said. Her words were followed by a silent stare that she was determined not to break first.

"What are you going to do now? Kill her?"

"You are too young to understand," Alice

deflated.

"Make me understand mom."

Alice looked down at her red nails.

"When you have been married for as long as your father and I have been, divorce kind of becomes pointless. It doesn't make sense to break up the kind of wealth and assets that we have acquired together." She rubbed her hands against each other, taking a moment to pause before continuing. "It also doesn't make sense to let harlots and their children inherit from it."

"Hm?" Mmakoma.

"I worked too hard to let a loose woman take anything away freely," Alice said.

"It's just one innocent child mom."

"If only you knew."

"What do you mean?"

"If I didn't do what I do, you'd have nothing left for you and your children."

Mmakoma breathed in to slowly take her mother's words in. Alice started laughing.

"What?" Mmakoma.

"The nerve to file a protection order against me," Alice said.

There was fresh air coming in from the opening that led to the balcony. The leaves of the fiddle leaf plant on the side were shaken by the wind that was coming in.

"I would do the same if I were her. In fact, I'd

open a case against you mom."

"It's not in her interest to get me arrested. Who's going to give her money when I'm behind bars?" Alice.

"Dad?" Mmakoma almost said dah! Alice laughed again.

"Your dad doesn't play like that," Alice.

"It's his child," Mmakoma.

"There's a reason she came looking for me and not your father," Alice said.

Mmakoma placed her hand on her cheek and fixed her eyes on her mother.

"You now know things I've protected you from knowing. You are going to act like a big girl and not make it awkward for any of us. You here me?"

"Yes mom," she agreed.

Alice picked up her bag and gazed into her daughter's eyes one last time. Mmakoma looked down, then back at her mother.

"Mom, do you remember where Aunty Tsakani's home was?"

"No, I don't. Why?"

"I've been thinking about her lately," Mmakoma.

"I had her home address somewhere in my files," Alice said.

"If you can find it, please send it to me."

The last patient for the day was a man in his fifties. He was a man of many tales, and he kept her engaged until it was too late to catch her daughters before they left for school holidays with Lekau.

When she got home, she immersed herself in a bathtub filled by bubbles. A glass of wine was by her side with a vanilla scented candle. She had never particularly found any joie de vivre from scented candles, but it looked pleasing to the eye. She supposed it was enough.

She wrapped herself with a cream towel and walked to the kitchen to return the wine glass. Khabonina was packing a stack of books left by the kids in the living room.

"Khabo, how are your kids?" Mmakoma asked.

"They are fine," Khabo's face lit up in parental pride. "My boy's soccer team won a tournament. He came home with a medal yesterday."

"Why don't you go home and see them? I will book a flight for you," Mmakoma said, realising that in the four years that Khabo had worked for her, she had never asked about her children. She would catch details here and there, but she had never shown any interest what-so-ever in the children of the woman who gave up time with her own children to come and raise hers so far from home. She had always thought that paying her well was enough compensation for her sacrifice.

Her mother's visit two days ago left her

wondering what being family truly was. She grinned at the issues that were known secrets between them, never discussed but shoved under the carpet and protected with the highest care.

"Serious?" Khabo was exhilarated.

"Go and see your children," Mmakoma said, browsing for the soonest flight to Durban. Khabo was to take a taxi from Durban to Umbumbulu thereafter.

She now had the house to herself for the first time in a while. She began to clean and move furniture around, desiring something new. A painting, a plant or maybe new curtains. She parked the thought for later as she wiped dust from the coffee table. She had forgotten how much comfort cleaning her house gave her. Khabo was always there to take care of it. If she wasn't there, there would be someone from the cleaning company.

She found Kamano at the entrance as she returned from a jog around the neighbourhood at twilight. He was still in his soccer gear from soccer practice. He drove in while she concluded her last few metres.

Typically, he came out of the car with a white plastic bag in his hand.

"At this rate, you're going to make me so fat I

won't even be able to come out of the door," Mmakoma jested.

"Rather that than you be so thin that the wind blows you away as you jog," Kamano.

"You know I never cared much for food until you came along."

She unlocked her door.

"We have versatile taste buds for a reason. Food must be enjoyed."

She excused herself for a quick shower while he browsed through her television for sports. When she returned to join him, he opened the white disposable, exposing the pap, spinach and braai meat.

"The other one has cabbage and tripe. Which one would you like?"

"Let me get plates first. We are not at the office." She rose.

"How have you been since…" he intentionally paused to allow her to fill the gap.

"I've been okay," she said.

"Boikarabelo says you haven't been yourself lately."

Something in how he said his words made the question in the statement obvious.

"I'm just tired."

"I can imagine," he ate a piece of meat. "And Naledi? How is she?"

"I don't know."

"I thought you would have checked her," he said.

"It's so complicated. I wouldn't know what to say to her," Mmakoma's eyes got teary. Kamano felt compassion.

"I hate what my mother did, but I also understand why she did it."

"Okay," he said, more to announce that he was attentively listening than to make any form of claim at understanding.

"I am worse than her," she said.

"Don't say that," Kamano.

"My mother does what she does for her own convenience. To save herself from public humiliation and to protect her years of hard work. But her hands are clean."

"Me on the other hand, I took my first baby's life. I have never been able to forget that," she cried.

"I can't even hand myself over to the police to pay for my sin because in the eyes of the law, there is no case. But my conscience has been shouting for justice ever since."

Kamano embraced her and let her shed her tears, making his soccer t-shirt wet all over his chest.

"Do you see why I am not good enough for a man with a pure heart like yours?" she said. Kamano wanted to make a joke of it but the look in her eyes made him know that she believed what she was saying.

"I never asked you to be perfect," he said. She

didn't say anything. But her face was covered in confusion.

"I want to spend all my life with you. That much is clear to me," he said.

"I've got so many issues Kamano. Don't you think I should first work on them before I get into the kind of relationship you want with me?"

Kamano's face dropped. He touched her shoulders, "I don't care about your issues. We will carry them together."

She started to cry. He held her tight in his arm and gently kissed her forehead.

"I hope you never leave me." She shook her head on his torso.

"I'm here, I'm not going anywhere," he said.

"I'm not the saint you think I am. I've done things Kamano," she mumbled.

"I know all those things. You've told me."

"And you still want me?"

"I don't just want you. I love you. You are far more precious to settle for just being wanted by me."

He held her tighter.

"That's intense."

"I mean it Doc."

"Why would you love someone like me? I'm red flags all the way."

"You are my match. A perfect fit for me," he said.

"And the woman who is still on the walls of your

house?" She raised her eyes into his.

"What about her?"

"Didn't you say the same thing to her?"

"Aw, you are jealous." He made puppy eyes, thinning his baritone. She bit her lip.

"Her purpose in my life was fulfilled."

He pulled away from her. "It took me so long to come to terms with that."

"Your house doesn't show a man who is over his late wife."

"You are right," he said. "I'll fix that, I promise you."

CHAPTER 16

He walked between the graves, reading the dates of birth and death of the people who once walked above ground. It was the first time since Lesego and their three children had been dug in and covered underground that he'd brought himself there.

He knelt by her grave and put a flower over it. This was the only place that Lesego had occupied that he had no flashback of. No memory of her in the place but just a brown casket going underground. He wondered what he would find if they were to remove the tombstone and dig. Would it be lifeless dry bones that didn't even look like her?

He moved to where his children were laid. He touched the stone with his hand and closed his eyes as the memory of the day he first became a father hit him. He remembered holding his innocent little girl in his hands as she cried at her first breath. He restrained the tears he felt in his eyes and pushed himself to read the words engraved on the tomb for the first time since her burial.

You have been a blessing. Goodbye my baby. May God take over from here.

Just a week shy of her tenth birthday, death came for her life and there was nothing anyone could do. She had been unable to keep her excitement about her upcoming birthday bated. Little did they know that Thabang Emelda Kgopa would not live long enough to make it to her tenth birthday.

Kamano shut his eyes for prayer, but no words came. He rose from his knee and went to the next grave.

Son of my youth, to have held you in my arms is a memory I will always cherish. Goodbye.

Those were the words on Khutšo's grave. Kamano wept. He was taken over by an overwhelming sense of weakness. What was a man without his family? He had nothing left to show for it. Death took everything. Not even the hope of grandchildren was spared for him. A legacy, his legacy was stripped away with no traces left except on photographs that no one will care to see.

A few years down the line, there would be no family tree with their names, no story to tell. And if he died, no one else would remember them.

You had just come to say Papa for the first time. I can never forget. I love you.

He placed the last flower on the baby's grave, working hard to suppress the wonder of how old he would have been now and what games he would be playing. Phenyo was his name.

He walked away from the cemetery and drove his VW Polo to his house. Not his mother's. His.

He pulled off the portraits on the wall. All the clothes, the toys, a cot and bottles, he compressed and stored in what used to be the nursery room.

A flashback of Lesego preparing it came to mind, it was a weak fading memory, but he remembered it well. That day, Thabang and Khutšo came into the house with muddy hands from the garden and touched the light blue curtain. Lesego wasn't too happy with them. How that memory had turned into a treasure in his mind was unfathomable.

He recited the verse Mrs Mabitsela had shared at school assembly the morning before:

Naked came I out of my mother's womb, and naked shall I return thither. The Lord gave, and the Lord hath taken away; blessed be the name of the Lord.

The reality of those words was striking hard. He understood Job, and only now was he truly beginning to mean it when he was saying blessed be the name of the Lord.

He pulled up his sleeves and cleaned over the

spotless house. It was somewhat satisfying to clean the house himself. There wasn't much to clean because a week after Lesego and the children's burial, he hired cleaners and gave them spares to go and clean once every month. Still, it was satisfying.

His phone was on the sofa. He picked it up and began typing.

Hi Mama. From now on, I'll be staying in my house. Thank you for being so kind in my difficult time. I love you.

Mavis called back instantly.

"Kgopa, what's going on?" she asked.

"I've decided to stop being a coward," he said.

"No, there's another woman, isn't there?"

"Maybe there is. But this has got nothing to do with her."

"Oh. Take care of yourself and come home to say goodbye properly," Mavis said.

"I'll see you later in the afternoon Ma."

"Good. See you then." Mavis hung up.

Kamano continued to clean his clean house. He packed everything that was a memoir of the life he once had, including his old clothes.

I'm going shopping this afternoon, care to join me? – he stopped to text Mmakoma.

Sure. I'm not working today. We can go- she

replied.

They went.

He picked up a baby blue short-sleeved shirt with two chest pockets at the store, he flipped it a few times before asking Mmakoma what she thought.

"There's no way I'm going with you anywhere with that," she chuckled. "It will make you look like Postman Piet."

"But this is nice." He defended his choice.

"Maybe for other people. I had a glimpse of you in this kind of shirt the day you acted like a hooligan at the traffic lights and no thanks, *nka loma postman*." (Cringing at the thought of the postman look- dir: I would bite the postman)

"That bad?" he laughed at himself.

"*Ka motshetshe, woo*," she cringed some more. (With an ironed crease on trousers)

"But you noticed me," he laughed.

"Forget it. I was irked out if anything," she laughed.

They concluded the shopping with a visit to a restaurant that had a deck overlooking an open bush.

"This is nice," she remarked at the calm of an open veld view.

"Is this the kind of place you like eating at?" he

asked.

"Never thought about it before. Maybe. It's nice," she said.

"Okay."

The waiter poured her a glass of red wine and served some warm lemon and water for him.

"You're a beautiful woman," he said. "In every sense of the word."

"Thank you," she smiled a fading smile.

"Do you think I can live up to her?" Mmakoma removed her eyes from his.

"You mean Lesego?" he searched for her eyes.

"Yes."

"No, you can never live up to her, even if you tried."

He paused, before touching her hand that was fidgeting with the serviettes on the table.

"You are brilliant in your way. Live up to yourself. Your best self."

She lifted her eyes again, "My whole life, no one has ever told me to live up to myself. Not even my parents."

Kamano's hand applied soft pressure to hers. He said nothing more.

CHAPTER 17

Her father was home in Bendor again. He was reading in his study. He stopped to look at her when she came in.

"Dad," she said. "I want to ask you something. It would help if you don't misunderstand me but acknowledge that it matters to me."

"Go ahead," he said.

There was always something ruminative in David Komane's face, even when he was being tender and warm. His dark brown skin and greying beard subtracted nothing to the kind of attention that would grace his entrance into a room. Matter of fact, it seemed to add to it.

"How many kids do you have?" Mmakoma asked. David Komane burst out in laughter.

"How many kids do I have?" He recited the question back to his daughter.

"How many siblings do I have?" she rephrased, waiting for her father to give her a straight answer.

"Five," he said.

"Five?" she couldn't conceal her shock. "Including the one on the way?"

"Yes, including the one you saved."

"You know about that?"

"I know everything." His husky voice deepened. Mmakoma welcomed the silence in between, opening the chair in front of him and sitting down. She began to track back to every word she had just uttered to her father. Her father had a way with words that forced her to revisit her thoughts. She wanted to ask him how he knew but decided not to. What she asked was enough for a day.

"How are things at Komane Civils?" She changed the subject.

"All good. We have new projects coming."

"That's nice, plus I'd love to get more involved," she said.

"How would you like to be more involved?"

"Haven't given it much thought, but I want to stop practising medicine."

She moved her eyes away to look at the bookshelf next to the window. Her father was an avid reader with a great collection of books that he was sometimes pedantic about. His office was a classic library, with tall bookshelves and brown furniture.

He didn't say anything, waiting for her to say more. She didn't. Instead, she stood up to leave him in the study.

"Would you like to meet them?" he asked her as she touched the door.

Mmakoma stopped and turned.

"How old are they?" She stepped closer to him.

He rose from his seat to get closer to her. He tucked her under his shoulder leading her towards the window that faced the landscaped garden outside.

"Wendy," he paused before continuing. "She' s seven years younger than you."

"Nhlanhla is twenty-three this year."

He moved back to his table and pulled out a pen and piece of paper and wrote down their names and numbers. He handed her the paper.

"Kganya and Tebogo are still teens," he said. "I'd have to facilitate the meeting."

"You know Wendy and Nhlanhla's numbers by head?" She was surprised.

"Just like I do yours," he said.

"Call them," he handed her the paper. "I'll tell them to expect your call."

"Wow dad, this is too much for me. I need to go and digest it."

She considered saving her tears for later when she got to her house. She used to not understand when people said that they needed to go home to cry but she was that girl now.

"I understand," David Komane said.

Mmakoma stood next to the window with her father by her side. The ease at which her father shared his other children had surprised her. More than that was the consternation of how the family she had known all her life was not what it was.

She decided to go past Cindy's place before going home. Nicolette, the woman who completed their trio, was back in Polokwane after a year of working abroad. They had planned to meet for an afternoon of catching up over wine and champagne.

Nicolette had the warmest of hugs that always went with a beautiful scent. Her body was soft and ambrosial, always. Even Mmakoma herself, who wasn't a typical hugger loved Nicolette's hugs.

"Did I miss anything noteworthy?" Nicolette asked as she arrived.

She put her hands in the platter plate that was on the table and took a bite of spicy biltong. (Dried meat)

"Not much on my part. But this one," Cindy giggled looking in Mmakoma's direction.

"What?" Mmakoma giggled.

"Are you going to tell her, or should I?"

"Oh please, there's nothing to tell," Mmakoma.

"She's been going about town with the hottest

high school teacher in all of Polokwane," Cindy giggled again, touching her nose with a hand that glistered in red nails.

"I thought you didn't like him," Mmakoma said.

"That doesn't take away the fact that the man is noticeable." Cindy gave Mmakoma a silly playful look.

"Mara a teacher MJ? Are sure he isn't here for a ticket out of poverty?" Nicolette.

"Y'all are annoying. He's a principal. He's doing fine. He didn't even know who my dad was when we met."

"He can't even get you a Birkin bag. Or surprise trip to Thailand at least," Nicolette.

"Guy even stays with his mom, imagine," Cindy jested.

"Y'all are mean hey," Mmakoma.

"Don't catch feelings with this one," Nicolette said.

"Too late because I really like him," Mmakoma said offhandedly.

"Wow," Cindy clapped her hands and tittered.

"I must meet him," Nicolette said.

"As long as you'll be nice to him," Mmakoma.

"Of course," Nicolette got up for the bathroom. She had put up a couple of kilograms, but none seemed to have gone to her waist. Like most South African women, she had the classic hour-glass shape of Saartjie Baartman.

The conversation between the old friends flowed effortlessly into the night. It made sense for them to sleep over.

Mmakoma was grateful for her light fading headache the next morning. She'd had worse hangovers. She rose before the other ladies, took a shower and promised to see them later. She drove to her apartment for a fresh set of clothes before heading to the hospital.

The underwhelming feeling that came with lack of purpose in her career of choice took over her mental space as she walked into the practice. It was something she could neither distract herself from nor shake off anymore. She had desired to make a name for herself. Something that had very little to do with the successes of both her parents.

She remembered the sense of pride that filled her when she first opened the practice. Patients came from as far as Thohoyandou, Musina and Bushbuckridge to see her, and it made her a proud doctor. The success she had worked hard to find was taking shape. Finally, a name for herself.

Success as a cardiologist was something outside of her parents. No one could credit her parents for the outstanding doctor that she was.

Now, her heart was no longer there. That box was ticked. It brought a set of ups and downs, survivals and deaths, tears and joy, but she desired more now. She desired purpose.

Practising in the most purpose-filled career was now something that left her feeling depleted. No part of her had desire to see a patient, even if it was just one more. Her heart had left the most coveted career path, medicine. Her certificates on the wall were evidence of hard work and commitment.

She pulled the first one she ever got and hugged it. She remembered the feeling she had when she walked on that stage, her parents sitting proudly on the audience. Her grandmother was still alive, and she graced her walk with ululations and sereto (clan/family praise poem).

Ke Mokone wa ga Komane,

ke wa ga mmammodu a temong a mokwa senkgopotsa balemi bahumagadi ba dutse... (Komane clan praise poem)

The old woman had recited the praise poem with pride, wearing a maroon traditional garment worn by Northern Sotho people. Her head was covered in a black beaded headdress, signifying seniority.

Alice hid her eyes as the old woman proudly praised her granddaughter in the graduation hall, having no care for boundaries and foreign protocol. Mmakoma smiled at the memory of it.

Charlene interrupted with a knock at the door. She asked Mmakoma how she was.

"I'm thinking of closing the practice."

She dropped the bomb on her. Charlene's smile turned into a worried frown.

"I will find work for you before I close. I know people who'd be happy to have your services," Mmakoma said.

She knew how Charlene's grandfather's farm had become unprofitable and not much success had come with trying to sell it. With the talks of 'expropriation of land without compensation' that were said everywhere on media and social media, Mmakoma was aware of the threat to whatever livelihood the Van Dyks' still had.

"Thank you."

Her face gave away the worry in her mind.

"We are going to see all the patients who already have appointments with us. Then we will transfer them to my doctor friends going forward," Mmakoma said.

Charlene didn't find the closure surprising. She had watched Mmakoma struggle for some time, and it was only natural to put a stop to it.

The first patients for the day came in. Mmakoma wore her best behaviour and served them the best way she knew. Kamano surprised her with a visit at noon. Like always, he had food. He softly knocked on her door and let himself in. Unlike on other days, this time he wore blue jeans that lacked the typical geometry. He also had a white golf t-shirt and a sleeveless jacket. It was a look that took Mmakoma by surprise. Pleasantly so. Although they had shopped for the clothes together, he had refused to do fittings.

"You look,… different," she smiled. "In a good way."

"Just compliment me straight. Tell me I look good."

He spun around before sitting down.

"You look good," she smiled shyly.

"I wanted to see you yesterday, but I couldn't get you on your phone," he said.

"Oh, I was at Cindy's place and my battery died," she explained.

"Please text me when your phone is about to go off. I can't afford to worry like that, especially after the farm…"

"I'll try."

She took a bite of the spicy mogodu. (Tripe)

"Your friend, Cindy is…" he paused to stop himself from saying more.

"What about her?" She sensed a need to be defensive.

"I don't think she's good for you," he said.

"Aargh come on Kamano. You want to tell me who my friends should or shouldn't be and you've been my boyfriend for how long? Two minutes?" Mmakoma breathed and opened her eyes wide.

"Am I?" Kamano smiled.

"What?" She was dumbfounded.

"Your boyfriend."

His baritoned chuckle came out hilariously,

making Mmakoma laugh too. She rolled her eyes sheepishly.

"It must be these new clothes," he joked.

CHAPTER 18

Charlene brought Mmakoma a cup of tea with her diary. Mmakoma thanked her for the gesture and began to playfully draw flowers on the page. The date grabbed her attention. She could never forget it. The 15th of October.

It was as clear as day in her mind. She circled the number a few times before pulling out tissue to wipe her tears. She had watched Aunty Tsakani drop to the ground and become lifeless on the day, years ago. It was just the two of them at home. Her mother was away on business and Aunty Tsakani had been saying that her body wasn't feeling too well.

She dropped her backpack and ran towards her

but she was unable to say anything. She wailed inaudibly, holding her chest tight and becoming weaker with every second. Teenage Mmakoma ran for the phone, then sprinted back to try everything her mother had taught her about emergencies. It didn't help. She continued to lose her life before her eyes and by the time an ambulance arrived, Aunty Tsakani was no more. Her heart had failed, they later found out.

Drawing yet another childlike pattern of circles on her diary, she remembered the sticky note that she had written the address that her mother gave her. She searched her table for it. It was stuck underneath her calendar. That pleased her because it could have easily been in the rubbish bin.

She hadn't expected her mother to make the effort to check and give her Aunty Tsakani's address. Aunty Tsakani wasn't her favourite thing to discuss.

That Saturday, she got on her car and drove from Polokwane to Giyani. Kamano called her whilst she was on the way. He had a soccer game and had asked her to wait for him, but she could no longer postpone the trip.

Giyani looked different. The home was different from how she remembered it. Where there was a thatched rondavel (cone and cylinder African house) was now a cream house with stone decorations. She asked someone, a passer-by who was pushing a wheelbarrow if the Vukeya family lived there. He confirmed that the Vukeyas lived in that house.

Mmakoma regulated her nerves with a few heavy breaths. She pushed the gate and walked into the yard, praying that there would be no dogs to confront her. She hated being touched by animals. She hated their natural stench.

She went around the house and her eyes met those of a woman carrying a yellow bucket of water. It was one of those buckets that carried oils twenty-five litres of oil, typically for restaurants and eateries. The green paint was still there but most of it had faded, so were the few letters left on the bucket. Only the word foil at the end and the S at the beginning were still visible.

"*Thobela,*" she greeted. (Greetings in Northern Sesotho)

"*Ahee, minjani?*" the lady replied. (How are you in XiTsonga).

She directed her with her hands to take a seat on the short embankment wall that is typical of villages in Limpopo. The wall was made to be a lapa with a step for sitting. A large family group could sit together outside without need for a chairs.

"My name is Mmakoma," she started. "I'm looking for the late Tsakani Vukeya's home."

The woman looked puzzled. It was a heavily silencing puzzle. A piercing shock.

"Did you know her?" Mmakoma.

"She was my mother," the woman said.

"Are you Nkateko?" Mmakoma's face lightened up.

"I am. Who are you?" Nkateko asked.

"I'm Mmakoma," she replied. "Your mom raised me."

"Woa, you've grown so much," Nkateko laughed.

"You have grown so much." Mmakoma.

"Let me get you something to eat," Nkateko rushed into the house without giving Mmakoma a chance to decline. She smiled at the sentiment. Aunt Tsakani was the same.

Nkateko came with a tray loaded with a teapot, two cups, three cans. One with sugar, another with teabags and the last with powder milk. There was also a plate with scones on the side.

She placed the tray next to Mmakoma and rushed back into the house. She came back with a kettle and poured over the teabags she had put in the teapot.

Mmakoma felt like she was about to hang out with an old friend to exchange gossip. She smiled and thanked her.

"My mom always talked about you when she came back home," Nkateko said.

"Really? I hope it was only good things," Mmakoma laughed.

"I only remember the good things," Nkateko said.

"I miss her so much," Mmakoma said. Nkateko kept quiet for a moment and sipped tea and chewed her scone. The scones were soft, moderately sweet and creamy to the taste.

"Death is wicked. I always hoped my mom would come back home and be with me for longer, but she left too soon. I miss her too," Nkateko said.

Mmakoma began to feel a sense of guilt. For sixteen years she went back and forth in her prayers. Why would God take away the only woman who ever loved her? The only woman who ever made time to listen to her and care for her needs.

Not once in her life had she ever stopped to ask herself what it took for the woman to raise her. It took time away from her own daughter. Time that could never be gained back. A loss that could never be amended.

"I'm sorry," she said to Tsakani.

"We both lost an amazing woman," Nkateko said.

"Do you have any children?" Mmakoma asked to evade the teary atmosphere that was building up between the two of them.

"Yes, two girls," she said. "They were here not so long ago. A friend of theirs is having a birthday party today."

"I also have two girls," Mmakoma giggled.

"Girls are nice to have. They take care of you when you're older," Nkateko.

"Yeah, they do," Mmakoma said, biting her scone again and welcoming the calm of the village and the sound of cattle bells.

It was a hot day but something about that part of Giyani was still so remote and raw, untouched and unscathed. She fell in love with it again. It was home.

CHAPTER 19

When she told Kamano that in the coming week she was to make a trip to see Wendy, his face immediately turned awry.

"Are you sure you're alright?" he asked.

"Last week it was Giyani and now you want to go to Hammanskraal?"

"I need to do this."

"I'm going with you."

Mmakoma had second-guessed herself from the moment she picked up the phone to call Wendy. She did it anyway. It felt like betrayal to her own mother. But it was what it was, Wendy was ready for her.

She took out some chairs when Mmakoma and Kamano arrived at her one room rented backyard apartment in Hammanskraal. They sat outside, under the shade of a tree and Mmakoma introduced herself.

"I came here to see you because I have just found out that I have a sister," she said.

"Oh,' Wendy gave a neutral response. Enough to encourage Mmakoma to keep talking but also too dry to be welcoming.

"Our father told me about you. I wanted to meet you," Mmakoma said, trying to fill in the gap that would have made the meeting more unwieldy.

"I've read about you," Wendy said.

"Really?"

"I've always wondered why he kept choosing you over us."

"Oh," Mmakoma sighed speechlessly.

"I still wonder," Wendy.

"I'm sorry," Mmakoma.

"Don't apologise, it's not your doing," Wendy said. Mmakoma looked into her palms trying to find suitable words to fill the gap.

"I appreciate the fact that you came here. It says a lot about the kind of person that you are," Wendy said.

"I don't drink tea, so I don't have it. Only beer in my fridge," she giggled.

"Don't fret, we already had something on our way here."

"I will get you cooldrink," Wendy said, pulling out

a small wallet from her tracksuit pocket.

Her feet were in cream flip-flops. They were covered in the red dust of Hammanskraal.

"Kamo," she called out and a child appeared from the other side of the landlord's house. The child didn't look like she had been through a bath of water that day. Her clothes were brown in dirt.

"Take a bottle next to the fridge and get us cooldrink," Wendy said, before turning her face to ask Mmakoma and Kamano which flavour they wanted. They both said coke and the child ran to the shop.

"Does dad come to see you?"

"He does sometimes. But you know how he is. I have to be clean and sober every time he comes, so I give him excuses sometimes," Wendy laughed.

Mmakoma smiled at how that sounded much like her father. He hated it when women drank alcohol.

"Is that your daughter?"

"Yes."

"She's a nice child," Mmakoma said.

"She is. I try my best with her," Wendy said.

The little girl came back with a bottle of Coca-Cola and handed some change to her mother. She went into the one room and came out with two glasses on a small tray. She rinsed them on the tap outside the curtsied to hand a glass to Kamano and Mmakoma.

"Thank you," Mmakoma smiled at her.

The girl looked like she was nine or ten years old. A year or two younger than Mogau.

"Can I go and play now Mama?" she asked Wendy.

"Before you go, this is your aunt, Grandpa Dae's daughter. My sister," Wendy said.

"And this is her friend."

"I didn't know Grandpa Dae had a daughter. He's so cool. We always meet him in the best restaurants," the little girl was pleased.

She hugged Mmakoma and Mmakoma hugged back. The little girl's dirt bothered her, but she tried to hide it. The girl ran off, leaving them to engage in grown-up conversation.

David Komane's daughters promised to keep in touch with one another and Wendy opened her arms and hugged Mmakoma. Helpless tears went out of her in the embrace of a sister she never knew she had.

"Bye." She wiped her tears with her hand as she found Wendy's warm smile.

The drive back to Polokwane was reflective on her part. She was grateful not to be the one behind the steering wheel and forced to focus on the road. Her mind was elsewhere. On her parents. On the wonder of who they were outside of being her mother and father.

Kamano complained about being hungry as they got off the N1 to get into Polokwane, and eventually her place.

"I made some bolognaise this morning. Unless if you want something else to eat," she offered.

"Bolognaise sounds nice. I'd love that," Kamano said.

He waited for the traffic light to turn green before turning left.

Khabonina was watching something on TV when they arrived. She mentioned something about a friend in town and left the house immediately. Mmakoma knew that she was using the time to go and see her boyfriend.

"When are your children coming back?" Kamano asked picking up the remote control.

"Tomorrow," Mmakoma replied, placing a scoop of mince on top of spaghetti. She handed him a plate and sat next to him.

"You cook well for someone of your kind," Kamano said as he rolled some spaghetti for a mouthful.

"My kind?" She turned.

"What? I'm being kind to even say your kind," he laughed.

"What kind is my kind?"

"I don't want trouble woman. I'd rather not say." He laughed more.

"I'll just hang on to the compliment and forget your shady undertones."

"Smart girl."

One of the teams on TV nearly scored a goal, making Kamano rise halfway from his seat. She laughed at him. Then she quietly focussed on her phone.

"Are you okay?" he patted her thigh, his eyes glued to the screen.

"Yeah, yeah. Just thinking about my newly found sister."

"What about her?" Kamano took down the TV sound.

"Just like me, she hides her drinking from dad," Mmakoma smiled tenderly.

"You might have fooled your father but her? Hai, no. Your dad knows."

Kamano restrained laughter.

"Don't be like that," Mmakoma laughed.

"You know she said something that kept me thinking on our way back." She stopped laughing.

"She said that she always wondered why dad kept choosing me over her. The truth in her words is hard to take in."

Mmakoma rubbed the side of her nose.

"Hm," Kamano sighed.

"Who are we outside of the small world we get to see?" Mmakoma asked rhetorically. Kamano said nothing to add to her words.

"Maybe it's time to tell Dipuc who her father was." There was comfortable silence before Kamano broke in.

"Have you thought about it thoroughly?" he said.

"I think so."

"It's a very serious thing babe. You need to be sure."

Mmakoma smiled at him. He didn't call her Doc.

"Don't smile like that, I mean it," he said.

"You just stopped calling me Doc. I could do with my new pet name."

"What name? Babe?"

His face became tender. She moved closer to him and hugged his muscular arm. He pulled it out and used it to cover her shoulder.

"I like having you around," she said.

"Me too." He touched her expectant face with one of his hands.

She gripped on to his neck and plucked her lips onto his. He turned his upper body and drew her even closer to him. She reclined her body, softly pulling him over her. He unzipped the back zip of her blouse and unravelled her bra loose.

"We need protection. I have it in my handbag," she whispered.

He stopped kissing her and looked into her eyes before pulling her top to cover her.

"I should go."

He stood up and fixed himself. Mmakoma watched him pace for the door.

He was gone.

She cried.

CHAPTER 20

Kamano was quiet. No text, no call and no visit. The next day went by, then the one after also passed. He was like a ghost. Had they gone all the way, she would have blocked him by now. She hated men who did that.

But Kamano ran before the act. She was hurt still. Why? She wanted an explanation. If there was any, she had to hear it before blocking him.

She had promised herself that she would never again let any man share her bed then leave her broken. She had promised herself that she would never again be any man's booty-call. She was no longer one-night-stand material. And if by chance it happened, blocking a man from contacting her wouldn't erase what they did. It wouldn't erase how it truly left her feeling. But it gave her a feeling of control. That was victory in a way.

None of her experiences had ever prepared her for a man who runs away from physical intimacy. Not once had she heard of it.

"Doc," Kamano said on the other side of the long-awaited call.

"I'm sorry."

Her stomach tightened. She wanted to fight him. She wanted to vent, to argue to brawl, to release the tension she felt towards him. He apologised too soon. It robbed her.

"Okay," she said.

"Thank you," he sounded relieved.

"Are we still on for the awards this Friday?"

"Sure," he said. She was just glad to still have a partner to attend the event with. Her father also wanted to host a braai at his house the next day. She would read the room at the awards to gauge if inviting him was a good idea. Especially where her mother was concerned.

Kamano arrived at the venue wearing a navy two piece. The shirt had a mandarin style collar with a red trimming on the chest pocket that hid inside.

She was surprised when they met at the parking lot. Perhaps the look was to suss her and make up for their last encounter. He was noticeable. He made an effort, great effort to dress up like that. And he looked like his effort. He was suddenly a man she would pick him in a room any day. The complete opposite of what she thought of him when they first met.

The Construction Industry Awards were graced by high profile politicians, businessmen and women, professionals, artists, musicians and notable industry players. Any sane businessperson wanted their name to be attached to the highly funded event.

Mmakoma placed her arm underneath Kamano's and made her way to the table reserved for her, her parents, the senior Makwelas, Tony Hastings, his wife and the deputy minister of trade and industry, Themba Mabuza and his young wife. On the table next to them was Masilo and Pogisho Makwela, the Mokoena-Andersons, the Potgieters and the Tinklers. She didn't expect that Lekau would be at the event. He had little if any involvement in the construction division of their family business. Masilo oversaw that.

They greeted and Alice had no care to hide her look of disapproval towards Kamano. It made Mmakoma uncomfortable because her mother had a bitter way with words when it pleased her. She could utter raw words and leave you to decide what you wanted to do with them. She prayed it didn't get there.

David Komane was talking to Caiphas Makwela.

The conversation seemed intense, something Mmakoma did not want to interrupt. They both stopped to acknowledge her. Her father gave Kamano a handshake before facing Caiphas Makwela again.

Afro Jazz, Afro beat and Afro Pop musicians entertained the audience, making the event enjoyable and less rigid. They were followed by a comedian, then the awards came. Komane Civils received an award for the most innovative road construction methods and use of plant. David Komane was particularly proud because it meant that their ways were going to be published in industry journals and included in project specifications, to be used and remembered throughout the country for years coming.

"We've got to do something for the team soon," he said to Mmakoma.

"Yeah, they did well in this," Mmakoma said.

"Had it not been for your mom persuading me to fund the experiment, we wouldn't be here." David touched Alice's shoulder.

"She's the one who came up with strategies and ways to conduct the experiment. She persuaded me to fund it and to get the necessary people involved. I married a genius."

His laughter captivated the table.

Mmakoma smiled shyly as David started a conversation with Kamano. They got very engaged in the conversation but what was remarkable was when he invited him to their family braai that was to be hosted in Bendor the next day.

An avocado green McLaren drove in and parked next to Kamano's VW Polo. Lekau came out of it. He had gotten himself a new sports car. His daughters knew the car. They were excited when they saw it. They ran up to hold him and speak endless babblings.

Caiphas Makwela was at the braai stand with David Komane and Kamano. Lekau went to join them and Mmakoma made a small prayer when she saw him. She hoped that nothing would turn sour between two of the men she had lied with. Technically not the latter, but they would have done it had he not been a coward that fled at the heat of passion. Her thoughts were loud in her mind, and she was glad that nobody could hear them. It was weird to have an ex with whom passionate memories existed and a current partner, with whom that area of memory is blank, empty, nothing to reminisce about.

She was in love with him anyway. It was a new kind of love for her. She was enamoured by his character and personhood, his way with words, the way he fed her, the way he joked and laughed, the way he could be strong and assertive, yet caring and reassuring. It was his righteous fear of God and not his robust rugby player body. He didn't dress too well for it in the beginning anyway. Even if he didn't have it, it wouldn't take away what she was experiencing with him. She touched her lips at the anticipation of the passionate love they stood to share.

Her aunt, Louisa came to sit next to her. She was complaining about the heat and that the pap wasn't yet cooked. Mmakoma smiled at her complaints. Very few people there would be bothered by the absence of pap. There was a variety of salads, rolls and finger food.

Aunt Louisa was Alice's sister. For the most part, they didn't get along. Mmakoma didn't know why her mother did not get along with her own sister and she had never asked. Aunt Louisa had two daughters, Matshediso and Seriti, and a son, Thato. She had never been close to any of them because of the drift between their mothers. This made them only see each other during family functions like weddings and funerals.

Only one of her father's three brothers had bothered to honour the invite, Rangwane Pule. The others sent apologies. She suspected that it had something to do with their wives who didn't get along with each other and with Alice.

Her father was the eldest of five siblings. Her late

aunt, her namesake, Rakgadi Mmakoma, was the second, then Rangwane Pule whose wife is late. After him are the last two who asked to be excused.

Her late aunt's son, Muvhuso was in attendance with his children. Their excitement at seeing their cousins, her daughters amazed her and warmed her heart. She entertained the idea of making a better effort to get to know Muvhuso's wife, Rachel.

Of her friends, Nicolette was also in attendance, but Cindy wasn't. She wasn't particularly proud of herself for having introduced Naledi to David Komane. Even though Alice didn't know that she was behind them meeting, it still it ate at her conscience, and she felt ill-prepared to look Alice in the eye.

"The pap is done," Nicolette came from the kitchen looking proud. She joined them on the garden chairs and looked at the men who were turning the meat and laughing in conversation. Alice and some of her friends were at the thatcthed lapa talking and laughing.

"So that's him."

Aunt Louisa threw a silly look at Mmakoma. Mmakoma glistered shaking her head up and down.

Aunt Louisa looked at her and clapped her hands laughing,"You still look at Lekau like that after having so long?"

Nicolette and Mmakoma looked at each other.

"It's not Lekau she's smiling about Aunty. Lekau

has a wife," Nicolette explained.

"Le re Lekau has a wife?" Aunty Louisa.

"He does Mmamogolo," Mmakoma confirmed.

"Eh," she clapped her hands again. "I thought the two of you were going to give us a big wedding one day. What happened?"

"Ai Mmamogolo, it's old news now," Mmakoma said.

"So, that one who's talking to your father is the one you two are talking about?" Aunty.

"Yes," Nicolette confirmed.

"Iyo, things of today, ai." Aunty clapped her hands one more time. "In our time, the father of your children would never be at an event with your boyfriend like this. Let alone a family event."

"Times have changed Aunty," Nicolette said.

"Ya, they have. Even your father. He wouldn't be so comfortable with it. Look at them."

She clapped more.

David sent one of Muvhuso's children to fetch a bowl. The meat was ready. The boy ran into the house and came out with a bowl. The men moved closer as food was being dished out.

"The meat looks nice," Alice said. The ladies all agreed.

"Let me dish up for everyone. I'm going to start with my daughter's number one," Alice said throwing a smile at Lekau.

His face expressed confusion, then a smile to

cover it as Alice handed him the plate.

"You had better not delay with the cows now, look at the nice food we make here," she joked. (Cows are used literally and/or symbolically as bride price) Kamano looked at Mmakoma. Mmakoma's eyes widened as she shook her face. She gently lifted her shoulders in confusion.

David pulled his wife aside and they started to talk with low tones. Mmakoma covered her face with both her hands and sat down as Lekau placed his plate on the table and asked to be excused. He left. Caiphas Makwela went up to shake David's hand and left with Rebecca.

David Komane led his wife into the house. Mmakoma followed them shortly afterwards.

"Alice you must stop manipulating situations like this. It has gone too far now," David was saying. They were in his study, but Mmakoma could hear them from the passage.

"Rich coming from you David," Alice said.

"I mean it Alice. You shouldn't have invited Lekau. I told you to leave the Makwelas out of this one," David said.

"They are family," Alice said.

"Kgopa is a good man. Lekau is a married man. Stop it," David fired the words with his husky voice.

"No daughter of mine will marry into poverty. Not under my watch," Alice said.

"He's not poor," it sounded like David Komane

was shaking his head. "Your daughter is better off happy than wealthy. Look at where all the wealth has gotten us."

"It wasn't the wealth, it was you David, it was you," Alice puled.

"What was I supposed to do? You shut me out all these years. You refused to give me other children. Damnit, you refused me my rights as a man, as your husband."

"Your rights over my body? Come on," Alice's voice was still shaking in anger.

"I loved you in every way I could. I still do. But you are stone cold," David said. He sounded like he was now seated.

Mmakoma walked out of the house to check if nobody else was close enough to hear her parents fighting. Everyone was at the lapa. She was relieved.

"I'm sorry," she whispered to Kamano as she passed next to him.

She could tell from the perspiration in his hands that he was no longer comfortable. He left without saying a word.

Monday evening, he came to the hospital with food. He was in his sports gear, after training.

He sat in her office waiting for her to return from

theatre. It was an office smaller than the one she used to have in her medical suite. She was to use it until her notice period would be fully served. It was plain and generic. There was nothing that made it her own except for a name at the door. Her medical rooms were now rented out to another doctor.

She was bewildered to see him, but his smile was reluctant, and dry. He opened the pack and took out her food, and his. He began to eat his pap, spinach and hardbody chicken, quietly.

"You seem to get along with my father," Mmakoma broke the ice.

"He's a wise man. I learn a lot from him," Kamano said.

"Did he ask you the proverbial question?" Mmakoma giggled.

"Which one is that one?"

"Your plans with her daughter," she chuckled.

"Not even. Ncaa, I was disappointed. The way I was prepared for the question, I was going to knock him off his socks, I'm telling you."

Kamano crossed his fingers and lightly laughed.

"And Lekau?"

"What about him?"

"Wasn't it awkward with him?"

"It was awkward. Very awkward. But I wasn't going to give him the satisfaction by being the first to leave."

"Eh," Mmakoma laughed.

"He was in my territory. I wasn't going to leave first."

"Oh, my word. You're even claiming territory," Mmakoma laughed at the thought of the unsaid conversation between Lekau and Kamano.

"He stepped into mine, some *ish* happened, it got a little ugly but still I wasn't going to cow out of it."

"Wow."

"When I saw him arrive at your father's house that day, I said to myself, *qhude manikiniki, zindala zombili*," Kamano had pride written all over his face. (a Zulu phrase to challenge an equal opponent).

"Wow," Mmakoma laughed softly. She was relishing at how territorial Kamano was. It made her feel like a damsel, ready for the rescue. No man had cared to mark a territory around her before.

"I'm going to come clean," she said as Kamano rose to wash his hands.

"Come clean about what?" Kamano asked.

"Dipuo," she said.

"Are you sure?" Kamano went down to his seat again.

"I'm not. But the truth is always better, isn't it?" she said.

"Not with this."

"What do you mean?"

"Have you thought about what it will do to Dipuo? And Mogau?"

"It's not going to be easy for them, but the secret is better out," Mmakoma said.

"Better for who?"

"For everybody," Mmakoma.

"No, certainly not for the kids. Nathaniel is deceased. Lekau knows the truth, I know the truth. Who will benefit from you complicating the kids' lives in pursuit of telling the truth?" Kamano.

"*Ai* Kamano," Mmakoma.

"I don't like Lekau. I probably never will. But he's been Dipuo's father. He's played his role and kept this secret like it was nothing. I don't see the benefit in confusing Dipuo now," Kamano said.

"And what happens in the future when she finds out?" Mmakoma turned her face sideways.

"Maybe she'll find out, or maybe never. But when she's older, in my view, she will be able to handle it better," Kamano said.

"I don't want to live with a secret hanging over my shoulder. I don't want to carry the fear of it ever coming out," Mmakoma said.

"I suppose you'll have to weigh your options," Kamano sighed. "But you can choose to not let it be a secret, but something you are prepared to explain to Dipuo if she ever hears it one day. If I were in your shoes, I'd prepare for that day instead. Not to shutter the world she knows now, for nothing."

Mmakoma looked at Kamano and breathed in hard.

"Think about it, be sure," he said. "Any decision you make, I will stand by you. But if you decide to tell her, consider that I'm also about to enter her world. We don't want to create additional parental issues and confuse such a happy child."

He held her hand and kissed it, then left. She was disappointed that he didn't go for her lips.

CHAPTER 21

The noise from her daughters arguing in the kitchen was her alarm that morning. It wasn't just one of those fights that she had gotten used to ignoring. They were shouting. They were screaming, and it sounded like they were about to handle each other physically. If it came to that, it was obvious who would win the fight, but somehow, Dipuo was ambitious, overly so, every time.

Mmakoma got off her bed and hurried on to keep the peace. Fortunately, Khabo was already on site, keeping the girls metres apart from each other and ordering them to silence.

"None of you will say anything," she commanded them. "Until you are calm enough to discuss the problem, you will both keep quiet."

The girls obeyed and continued moving about in their morning routine. Mmakoma smiled at Khabo and turned back to her bedroom. She had been able to enjoy hours of good sleep since her last working day at the hospital. The fatigue that she had gotten used to carrying around for years on end had finally weaned itself off from her body. And in the same strength was the inescapable pull to adapt to the petty fights between her daughters and the endless conversations they demanded.

It was just a day ago when Khabo called Mogau out for fighting with Dipuo over a triangular toy, "You are older. Give it to her."

"That's not fair," Mogau was enraged. She pushed the door of Mmakoma's bedroom and stormed in unannounced. She was about to say something to Mmakoma, but she didn't. She just stood there in her school uniform. A scotched blue skirt and white golf t-shirt.

Mmakoma felt like hugging her but decided against it. She didn't want to validate victory of an argument she knew nothing about.

The latest argument was much louder, more fiery, and most passionate. She knew about sibling rivalry but never had she imagined that the fluctuations between war and love would be so frequent.

She turned back and went to her bedroom to shower. The water was tender and warm, reminding her of the cuddle of a man. It had been a long, long time, and Kamano was too slow for her peace of mind. What is the point of having a man if you aren't even getting any time between the sheets? She hit the faucet and the supply of water stopped.

She dressed up and walked back into the living areas and found her daughter still sombre over their fight.

"Ready for school?" Mmakoma asked. Mogau nodded.

"I'm taking you to school today," Mmakoma said. Mogau sprinted up in sudden excitement. Mmakoma was surprised to see the speed in which her daughter's face lit up.

"Dipuo, Dipuo, mom's taking us to school today." She ran to her little sister.

"Mom, are you taking us to school today?" Dipuo's glimmering face was expectant and seeking assurance.

"Yes," Mmakoma replied.

"Yeah," the two girls hopped in contagious excitement. Mmakoma felt at her happiest too.

Her week was spent between drop offs and pick-ups, something she never imagined herself finding pleasure from.

Nicolette and Cindy visited that Saturday.

"You've really resigned? I can't believe it," Cindy said. Khabo had gone to see her friends, and they would probably gossip about the madams while the kids were at the Makwelas. They told her that their grandmother was going to take them to a horse riding and polo event when Reneilwe arrived to fetch them.

"If I knew that taking my kids to school would be as nice as it is, I would have done it a long time ago," Mmakoma said, pressing down her kettle to boil water for tea.

She poured some for herself and offered her friends champagne. Rooibos tea was now the kind of drink she preferred the most. It had a way of calming her into sleep much quicker than wine without the subtle headache the next morning. She loved being able to match the kind of energy her daughters would bring into her new morning routine.

"I guess you are ready for the rich housewife life now." Nicolette strutted her champagne glass in the air in a celebratory tone.

"I never thought I'd ever see Mrs Medicine relax like this," Cindy laughed, picking a slice of pizza from the box next to her.

She was right. Mmakoma had never thought of herself domesticated. Not even in her wildest imaginations. The idea of a woman dropping her career and goals to raise her children was outdated and foreign to her before.

"It must be the new man."

Nicolette jiggled her shoulders, excited by her own words.

"After God, fear men. These roughnecks will domesticate you so quick," Cindy said.

"I hope he's not the reason behind you suddenly deciding to focus on motherhood," Nicolette said. "That guy hasn't got the money to support a high maintenance girl like you."

"At this point, I might just ask you to keep him out of your mouths because, wow," Mmakoma.

"He's your man for now, that means that he's our business. We will talk about him until he's not," Cindy said jokingly. Mmakoma rolled her eyes and sipped her tea.

"Look at you resisting wine," Nicolette laughed. "Did he also tell you to stop drinking?"

"He must have," Cindy fed the joke. She and Nicolette laughed hard at their wine-loving friend.

"But the guy looks like a snack. I love the fact that he's a big guy with all the muscles in the right places. Perfectly sculptured," Nicolette raised her glass.

"Fine specimen," Cindy added.

"Aowa, y'all are just going to discuss my man like I'm not here," Mmakoma said.

"How's he like in the bedroom?"

Nicolette ignored Mmakoma's protest. Her

question was exciting her, only to be met by an empty face.

"Don't tell me that he hasn't tasted the forbidden fruit," Nicolette opened her eyes wide. Mmakoma's face was still empty.

"Oh, my word, he hasn't," Cindy laughed.

"What's the point of all that physique if you haven't put the real thing to the test?" Nicolette.

"The manhood, you mean," Cindy. They filled the room with laughter.

"Some of us are stuck with potbellies," Cindy's words were mixed with laughter. "And you get one of the most sculptured men in all of Limpopo, but you deny him."

"It won't be long before he runs," Nicolette.

"I wish I was the one denying him," Mmakoma.

"What?" Cindy.

"He's the one that runs away when things warm up," Mmakoma.

"You don't say…" Cindy was in disbelief. She clapped hands with Nicolette like a piece of hot news just landed in her ears.

"You are serious?" Nicolette read Mmakoma's face.

"I don't know what to do anymore," Mmakoma said.

"No man runs from it. That's not normal," Cindy.

"Are you sure everything functions?" Nicolette enquired. Mmakoma giggled softly to her friend's words, covering her mouth.

"I've felt it rise. I think it works," Mmakoma.

"Janet you're serious, ne?" Cindy.

"And you really like him ne?" Nicolette.

Mmakoma nodded her head like a child.

"I wish I could give you tips but I've never come across a man who runs from the deed," Nicolette.

"Even the grandpas make sure they get pills or something. Running? Never ever," Cindy.

"And he likes talking about marriage," Mmakoma moaned.

"Girl, please don't ever do that to yourself. You can't vow forever with someone you've never tasted. No way," Cindy.

"Forever is a long time. Too long for bad sex. Don't do it," Nicolette.

CHAPTER 22

The under sixteen boys were in training that Friday afternoon. Thabo Maila too. Kamano was impressed by his ball control. He was the type of player that big teams scouted for. Kamano had high hopes for him with the tournament ahead. The boy had been working hard on his behaviour and academics. He was gradually gaining the type of discipline needed to make it as a professional.

He and James Mphela, their coach had had some conversations regarding his rare talent on the field. The whole team was exceptional. Kamano was proud to be their principal.

He was alone on the stands that afternoon watching them prepare for the tournament.

The feeling of his phone vibrating interrupted

him.

We need to talk- the message said.

There is something about those words that gets a man to shiver, even the boldest and strongest of them all. He placed his phone back in his pocket and threw his palms over his face.

"What's with you?" James asked, running into the field.

"Eish bro, women."

He rubbed his own head and tittered. He was in it. James laughed at him and ran into the field.

Thoughts fleeted through his mind wondering what the talk would be about. He continued watching the boys train. James shouted at two boys who were coming in late. His voice was strong and militant. Kamano smiled about it. His phone vibrated again.

I'm outside your house, you're not here. Where are you? – another message.

Kamano lifted himself from the stand and started to run. He waved at James who looked like he still had something to say.

Please wait for me, I'm on my way- he slowed down and typed. Not replying was going to get him into more trouble than he already was.

He found Mmakoma's car parked outside his house. The couple that lived next-door came out when Kamano arrived. He waved at them and pushed his gate open. He drove in and Mmakoma followed.

"Hi Doc," Kamano said coming out of the car with a reluctant smile.

"Hi," she said flatly.

He opened the doors and let her inside. He pulled a silent deep breath behind her in anticipation.

"What's her name?" she asked.

"Her name?"

"Yes Kamano, her name," she repeated, a little louder. Kamano laughed apprehensively.

"It's not a joke Kamano. Don't turn it into one."

"I'm not." He waved his hands in the air.

"I'm too old for your games Kamano. I've been played enough in my life and I have two daughters to consider."

"And I'm not trying to make you a fool Doc."

"You are. You don't even want to get close to me," she sobbed.

"Oh," he sighed relief and sat down.
"I should have told you this before."

"Shoot," she said fiercely.

"Nine years ago, I got myself into a horrible mess. I was caught cheating."

Mmakoma raised her face, surprised. She wiped her tears with her manicured hands.

"It hurt Lesego so much, but it also made me realise that I could lose my family for someone I didn't even like, like that," Kamano paused.

"Lesego was leaving me."

"She should have left you."

"She was."

"Why are you telling me all this? Once a cheater always a cheater *ha*?"

"Not anymore. I know what it took to rebuild my marriage. It took so much to let her heal and to have her trust me again. No one deserves the kind of pain she endured," he said.

"There was just no way we could have made it through that one except for God. We healed. We recovered and came out better. But it was a horrible time in my life. I'm not proud."

"What does that have anything to do with me now?" Mmakoma.

"I broke two women. I still don't know which is worse between cheating on my wife and breaking her heart, or getting into an affair, and letting the other woman think that she was special and that maybe one day I would leave Lesego for her."

"But why did you do it?"

"It started as a friendship. I was offering extra lessons for my students late in the day and she was doing the same. We'd stay after the lessons and talk for hours. Then I warmed up to her, and she warmed up to me. I started visiting her. I excused it as a friendship until we started getting intimate. It was fun, I mustn't lie."

Mmakoma was disgusted by it, her face showed it.

"I don't know how you women do it, but Lesego

found out, and caught me in the act. She was leaving me," he said.

"You had the other woman *mos*. You were going to be fine."

"You could say that. I also considered it. But in all truth, I didn't love her." He shook his head.

"Trust the brink of a failing marriage to get you on your knees begging God to save your marriage. You even make crazy promises like *'God, if you save my marriage, I will never, ever sleep with any other woman unless she's my wife,'*" he laughed.

Mmakoma laughed at him.

"Little did I know that I only had six years left with her," he said.

"Sorry," Mmakoma.

"I'm telling you all this to say that after Lesego's death, I thought it was over for me. I thought that I would never fall in love again. I was becoming okay with that. I had accepted it. Then I saw your fire, your passion, your drive, your confidence, your beauty and I said *hehehe, God*," he laughed.

Mmakoma blushed.

"I suddenly had a drive and a desire to live. To love again," Kamano said.

"But I vowed to God."

"Aargh please Kamano, you expect me to believe that?"

"I'm not lying," he said.

"You've got so many issues. Call me when you're

ready for a serious relationship with me, I don't have time for games," she stood up to walk.

"And I don't promise to be available then."

Kamano rested his face between his hands and watched her go. He considered following her, to beg her to forgive him and to stay. But what she wanted was more than he could give her. He bore the burden to be pure before his Maker.

For the longest time he battled with the verse that put fornicators and adulterers in the same basket with idolaters. It was easy to understand why idolaters wouldn't make it into heaven, maybe adulterers too. But two people who hurt no one? Seriously God? He had laughed a few times in unbelief over the verse in 1st Corinthians 6 verse 9 (KJV); *Know ye not that the unrighteous shall not inherit the kingdom of God? Be not deceived: neither fornicators, nor idolaters, nor adulterers, nor effeminate, nor abusers of themselves with mankind…*

But God said what He said and that was it. He felt restrained by it. He also felt washed, forgiven and made right every time he would read the words that followed.

And such were some of you: but ye are washed, but ye are sanctified, but ye are justified in the name of the Lord Jesus, and by the Spirit of our God.

He desired her, he wanted to give her his whole world, but this one thing he couldn't. Not after knowing what he knew. Not after vowing to be a man of integrity before God.

The love of this woman was sweet. She was passionate and fierce, yet so tender and fragile. It was obvious that she was gifted with healing hands, but he was healed by her laughter and purity of heart. She was bare before him. She kept nothing away from him. That was the highest form of purity, and innocence.

Mmakoma was amorous. She was breath-taking. He had battled to resist her many times. His mind was in chaos about it.

CHAPTER 23

Mmakoma watched her daughters drag their bags into the school premises. She was loving her newly found freedom to take her daughters to school, something she could never find time for before. Her mother had said that she would get bored and tired, but the girls always had a hundred things to say, and for her, that was enough.

She drove away from the school and went past a site that belonged to Komane Civils. The one that Patrick Zimba worked at. The last encounter she had had with the man was best forgotten. She decided not to enter the site camp, but rather observe activity from outside. They had progressed immensely since the last time she was there. At a different time, she would have asked for Patrick Zimba so she could congratulate him personally for his undeniable skill and exceptional leadership.

She went to her place and began to study the company's statements and returns on investments. She thought of ways that they could improve the company's brand and marketing. Contractors were not particularly known for marketing their companies well. They were tacky to say the least. Khabonina offered her tea. She thanked her.

She was going to talk to her father to consider releasing a budget for marketing, but that evening when she met with him at Bendor, business was the last thing he had interest in talking about.

"I spoke to Wendy earlier. It reminded me that I never asked you how it went with her." His statement was a question.

"It was okay. We have some things in common. We could hang out together I suppose," she said.

"She is a little rough around the edges, isn't she?" David laughed pleasantly.

"She is," Mmakoma.

"She would do with your mother's trimming and training." David laughed some more.

"You are so right dad," Mmakoma laughed even more, almost snorting.

"She says you came with a man. Was it Kamano?" David asked.

"Yeah," Mmakoma's face changed.

"What now baby?"

"We broke up dad," she said.

"That bast…" David breathed. "I'm going to break his bones. I told him."

"You told him that?"

"I said if he ever let a tear of yours fall down, he must call a chiropractor immediately." David banged his water glass against his table.

There was noise from Dipuo and Mogau. They must have been watching something hilarious in the living room.

"I hope you don't break his bones. He's too nice for that," Mmakoma said.

"Not with my daughter's heart."

Mmakoma looked at her father. There was nothing the man wouldn't give her, absolutely nothing. But Wendy's words filled her mind and made her feel guilty for being the apple of their father's eye. She was the one he chose to show to the world. She was his treasure, without doubt.

"Dad why do you keep choosing me over your other kids?" she asked him.

"I don't. Why do you say that?"

"They seem to think that you do," she said.

"Do you think that I do?"

"Maybe," Mmakoma said. "It doesn't matter what I think."

"It matters. Everything I do, I do it for you," David said.

"What about them?" Mmakoma.

"I've cared for them all their lives. I have visited them all their lives. They've always known me as a father."

"But does the world know you as their father?" Mmakoma.

"Does the world need to know me as their father?" David paused, pulling the kind of facial expression a parent gives to a child when explaining something.

"I'm not trying to get brownie points from the world. They need a father, that's what I have been." David was now looking outside.

"Is mom the reason behind all this?"

"Partially," he said.

"What do you mean partially?"

"I love your mother. She is my wife. We've been through many things in this life, but I love her." David Komane said. Mmakoma decided not to dig deeper, even though she found the answer unsatisfactory.

"I wish someone would love me, even with just a fraction of that kind of love."

"You must desire more. Not what your mother and I have."

Mmakoma's face expressed her unsaid question.

"You deserve better. Something higher and more sacred," David Komane added.

Mmakoma looked at the darkness outside the

window. She had so many questions about her parents and their marriage. It was becoming clear that they had done things to each other, possibly atrocious. But none would leave the other. The separate residences were making sense for the first time. They wanted to be close to each other and far from each other at the same time. Nobody else knew because in public they were a solid couple who inspired many. A power couple. They even gave marital advice to younger couples.

"How do I know if I've found the kind of love you're talking about dad?" Mmakoma asked. David laughed at her.

"Does he love you? Without doubt? Does he respect you? Does he see you in his future and unafraid to express it?"

"He says he does but he doesn't want to…" Mmakoma remembered that it was her father that she was talking to.

"He doesn't want to what?" David asked.

"You know."

It felt weird saying the words. David raised his brow seeming to get it.

"Is he seeing someone else?"

"I don't think so," Mmakoma murmured.

"That's a man with sexual discipline. Marry that comrade," David Komane laughed and left the room. Mmakoma held her mouth. Her father was hard to predict at times.

Alice Komane joined them for breakfast the next morning. Caiphas Makwela was coming to the house to discuss some business with David. It had something to do with the oil plant in KZN.

Mmakoma wondered if her mother was there to keep appearances or to genuinely spend time with her husband.

There was nothing unusual at the breakfast table. David and Alice spoke like they always have and laughed here and there. She hugged them and left after eating. She also left the kids behind because Caiphas Makwela was going to go back to Clearwater Cove with them anyway.

On her way to her place, she decided to take a detour for Kamano's house. Her mind went back and forth about calling first. She decided to just go.

She parked her car outside and pushed the pedestrian gate open. She knocked on the door a few times, then on the window. Kamano came to the window topless. He was surprised to see her there, and he rushed to the door to open.

"Doc," he said.

"Stop calling me Doc, I told you before," she insisted, letting herself inside. "And cover yourself, you're going to make it hard for me to talk."

He smiled like a teenage boy and rushed to get a

top. He wore it inside out unawares and sat on one of the chairs around the dining table, while she was on the sofa.

"I have a problem with you running every time we get warm," she said.

"I'm sorry," he interrupted her.

"I'm still talking. Don't cut me," she said.

"Okay," Kamano.

"I know about celibacy. I've never met anyone who practises it. Even the holiest of us." She pushed her weave backwards.

She was wearing black mommy jeans with a black vest. Smelling good, as always.

"I've certainly never imagined myself practising it. Not if I'm in a relationship," she went on. "But I can respect you for it. I can try. *Long* as you don't cheat on me."

"I won't."

She looked at him digging deep to check the sincerity of his words.

"What changed?"

He suppressed laughter while asking. He did badly at it. His words were laced with excitement.

"A chat with my father," she said.

"No, no, no Doc, you told your father about this?"

Mmakoma laughed at him.

"But it helped me see your choice as a strength, and not a weakness," Mmakoma explained.

"But still, how is he going to look at me now?"

"With respect…"

She pulled her brows up.

"I can't believe he knows." Kamano buried his head in his hands.

Mmakoma laughed at him. She went to get a bottle of water from the fridge.

He had done a lot to change the house. She had noticed it last time, but she was too frustrated to care.

"The chat with dad reminded me of what I wanted," she said.

"All my life I've lived a textbook life. I've done what was expected of me, never considering what it all meant. I wanted to please people and to be liked. I became a doctor because I wanted to please and to be liked. Yes, I've been off the wagon a bit, but that too was for others to like me."

"I love it when you're so serious," he joked.

"There's something you do so well, I don't know if you're aware of it or not."

"What is it? Fooling around?" he asked.

"Yes. You play a lot but there are things you will protect with everything you've got. That's attractive." Her voice was shaky.

"You only do what you love and what is meaningful to you, period." Mmakoma drew a line in the air with her hands.

"You have no idea how rare that is. I mean, I've

seen you around kids, you genuinely care about them and their future. It's not a coincidence that you're heading the best public school in all of Polokwane."

"Thank you," he said.

Mmakoma motioned her head in agreement and said nothing more.

"Are you done? I didn't mind hearing all these compliments," Kamano.

"I'm done."

Kamano rubbed his hands together like he was preparing to say something. Then he touched the helm of his top on the side. He looked at Mmakoma to check if she had noticed that his t-shirt was inside out.

She cracked up in laughter.

"And you don't tell me, *ai*," he complained, laughing at himself.

"Anyway, I wanted to be all serious and say that it's not good for me to be alone," he paused.

Her face was bright. It was beautiful. It radiated. The same way that his heart did.

"Please agree to join me. I will love you with all I've got. I will be a father unto your kids and everything a husband should be to you."

"Is this a proposal?"

"Yes, it is. Please agree to take this life with me. Be my wife, please."

Mmakoma swallowed the bout of saliva in her mouth and closed her eyes. She shook her head up and down before going into tears. Her whole body felt weak.

Could anybody still see beauty in her? Could anyone find her worthy? Could God let her, a sinner of sinners, experience something so beautiful?

She felt Kamano's towering presence close to her. He held her up and embraced her.

"You are a blessing of blessings to me. I thank God for meeting you because he has given me beauty in exchange for my ashes and anointed me with the oil of joy, for my mourning."

Dear Reader

My gratitude for you is greater than you can ever imagine. It warms my heart whenever I hear from someone who has read something that I have written. It humbles me.

I hope the stories that you have experienced in the series, *A journey back to purpose* have reached your heart in a special way.
Mmakoma and Kamano are people with many layers, like many of us. But the love of God reaches all of us and exposes us to the beauty of His open offer of salvation. I hope that Beauty for Ashes has reminded you of how God's offer is always the best, it doesn't matter the kind of mess and ashes you may be in.
My prayer is that we all find freedom from all the limitations that hinder us from living in purpose, and that we find victory over everything we face.

Now, is there anyone in this series whose story you'd love to read? Please feel free to let me know.

I'd like to end by saying thank you so much.
May God bless you.

Mapule Mokhawa